MOONLIGHT & MAYHEM

MYSTERIES OF MOONLIGHT MANOR

BOOK 3

MOLLY FITZ

TRIXIE SILVERTALE

Copyright © 2022 by Molly Fitz & Trixie Silvertale.

All rights reserved. Except as permitted under the U.S. Copyright Act of 1976, no part of this publication may be reproduced, distributed or transmitted in any form or by any means, or stored in a database or retrieval system without the prior written permission of the publisher.

Editor: Jennifer Jones, Book Ends Editing
Cover: Mariah Sinclair, The Cover Vault

This is a work of fiction. Names, characters, organizations, places, events, and incidents are either products of the author's imagination or are used fictitiously. Any resemblance to actual persons, living or dead, or actual events is purely coincidental.

No part of this work may be reproduced, or stored in a retrieval system, or transmitted in any form or by any means, electronic, mechanical, photocopying, recording, or otherwise, without written permission of the publisher.

Moonlight and Mayhem: Paranormal Cozy Mystery : a novel / by Molly Fitz and Trixie Silvertale — 1st ed.

[1. Paranormal Cozy Mystery — Fiction. 2. Cozy Mystery — Fiction. 3. Amateur Sleuths — Fiction. 4. Female Sleuth — Fiction. 5. Wit and Humor — Fiction.]

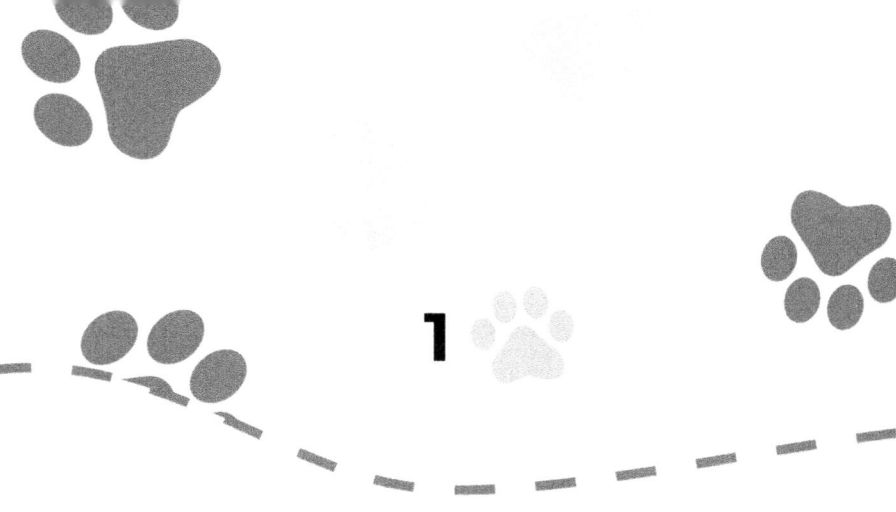

1

Third time's the charm. I'd heard that saying many times while growing up but never felt the weight of its scope until now. After my unceremonious exit from New York City, I began to rebuild my life in Misty Meadows. Somehow, after stumbling upon the deal of the century, I'd purchased a Gothic mansion called Moonlight Manor.

At the time of purchase, I hadn't known about the trio of residents I inherited when declaring myself mistress of the mansion. Hindsight being what it was, I doubted if knowing about them would have stopped me from making the manor my home. The place offered a fresh start I needed with a price tag that made it possible.

My realtor, Mia, had touted its nineteenth century

beauty. "The exterior is clad in rusticated granite and the front elevation is composed of two distinct towers. The one on the right is cylindrical and adds a little bump-out to the first floor drawing room and second floor main suite. The top of that round tower is trimmed with what's called egg-and-dart molding and capped by a conical Tyrollean roof. Technically, that's more of a Scottish Baronial feature, but because the home was built during the Gothic Revival period, it's still classified as Gothic."

Although, it wasn't until I ventured into the mysterious attic, hidden behind a solid door with an antique glass knob, that I fell in love with the place. Of course, loving it wasn't enough. I had to figure out how to make some money if I wanted to continue living with my three *ghostly* roommates. At least if I wanted to keep the lights on and continue eating. Not that my new friends cared much about either of those things.

Yet I didn't give up easily, and I had a head full of fabulous ideas.

Attempt number one had been a bed-and-breakfast, but after one of the most influential travel editors in the eastern United States skewered my property in a scathing review, that adventure crumbled. The travel editor didn't appreciate the nightmares and apparitions caused by the previous mistress of the manor being trapped between here and the hereafter.

Not to worry, my roots are solid, Midwestern stock. So I picked myself up and figuratively brushed the manure off—as I had literally done so many times on my father's pig farm. I'd learned the only thing between me and success was time and hard work, right? After we freed Beatrix de Haviland from her disquiet, she passed through to her final rest, and we were able to move on as well.

So I came up with idea number two in month number two. Since I shared my residence with three enterprising apparitions, two human and one feline, I opted to lean into the theme that presented itself. I set up haunted mansion tours for All Hallows Eve, and using my online marketing expertise, pretty much sold out for the season in four days.

Velma, Norman, and Sir Bogart, the beloved feline pet of Miss de Haviland, helped turn haunted Moonlight Manor into a thrill to behold. We were positioned to receive rave reviews for a new and blossoming business.

Unfortunately, on opening weekend, a real live—well, let me rephrase—an actual corpse turned up in my mudroom. So, that was Plan B down the toilet.

Here I am, once again brushing the dust from my hands and dungarees. All I needed now was an amazing Plan C.

Yes, this was most definitely a case of getting the girl out of Iowa but being unable to get the Iowa out of the girl.

I remained bullish, determined. Giving up, throwing in the towel, calling it quits? No way. Nuh-uh. Not going to happen.

We'd figure out a lucrative, workable idea. I was sure of it. Though, it would probably take all four of us to do so.

Seated nearby, the self-appointed Lord of the Manor, His Royal Felineness, Bogart the First, the Only, the Eternal, was a wealth of information. He'd been the best friend to a wealthy and influential costume designer during the Golden Age of film. He literally rubbed shoulders with some of the wealthiest families on the eastern seaboard, and in his ensuing years as a ghost, had accumulated knowledge in the areas of magic, manors, and antiques.

In the center of the drawing room, I hugged my mug of Velma's special tea to my chest to fend off the stress-ache forming there. "Sir Bogart, I was wondering if you could help me come up with a new plan to keep us afloat?"

His silky black fur glistened from within as he curled onto an ottoman and asked—no, *demanded*—to be placed in front of the fireplace in the drawing room. The winter wind sighed around the outside of the tower.

"Does the fire actually warm you?" I stared at the flickering flames, visible through his translucent body. The way the light refracted through his vaporous form mesmerized me.

He stretched lazily. "No, mistress. Although, the memory of such things keeps me from going mad."

His words reminded me of Velma's vicarious enjoyment when I described eating a caramel-apple cupcake to her. It had made her sad to be reminded of what she couldn't experience, but she had closed her eyes and tried to remember.

I took a sip of my tea and savored the mouth feel before I swallowed. Existing as a physical being did have its benefits. "I thought perhaps for our next venture, we could try something with antiques. I've learned a lot since purchasing the manor, and you seem to be a bottomless well of information on the subject."

He ignored my question and my flattery.

"Bogey, did you not hear me, or are you choosing not to answer?"

He rested his majestic head on a paw and stared at me with his all-knowing yellow eyes. "I heard you, mistress. However, I was pondering the wisdom of purchasing antiques, as you call them, to sell when you own a mansion full of them."

He had a point. "What are you suggesting?" I took another sip.

"Perhaps you, myself, cook, and butler could inventory the contents of the manor. There are certain things that will have sentimental value to the three of us who lived and died within these walls. However, I'm certain there will be a multitude of items which would fetch a handsome price if you were to locate suitable buyers."

For a moment, I forgot the brilliant feline was a ghost and attempted to stroke his back. My fingers drifted through his energy, but despite his lack of corporeal form, he seemed to purr.

"Can you feel that?" I asked, repeating the action.

"Once again, it is the memory—however distant—that brings me comfort."

Despite the slight twist in my chest from his words, I continued. "Well, I think you've had a wonderful idea. I'm going to run into town for supplies. Would you like a new toy while I'm out?"

His wide, glowing eyes closed to slits, and the nod of his head was nearly imperceptible.

When I'd arrived, mere months ago, his worn and tattered toys littered the attic. But in exchange for new and exciting forms of entertainment, we'd reached a détente. He offered advice, whether or not I asked for it, and I fetched him the occasional feathered plaything.

He closed his eyes all the way and remained stationary on the ottoman. "In your absence, I shall discuss the plan with Velma and Norman."

"Thanks. I'll be back in an hour or so. I'll probably stop at Heaven Can Bake and enjoy a coffee and some gossip with Frannie."

His eyes remained closed, but he hummed in agreement. "Safe journeys, mistress."

2

One benefit of living deep in a pine forest was the lovely contrast of evergreen needles against the building drifts of fluffy white snow. It was going to be a white Christmas, for certain. And unlike New York City snow, which was scraped into muddy brown-black piles and was nothing more than an inconvenience for designer shoes, this wonderful winter wonderland was full of promise and possibilities. How beautiful the pristine snow would be when it covered my fields. I shivered, not from cold, but from excitement. What would the next season hold for my manor?

The SUV I lovingly referred to as Blue Bell had a great set of snow tires, and even though I'd been without a car for seven years in the Big Apple, my driving skills were shaping up nicely. I had learned to drive early back at my hometown farm, but it was another item on the checklist of things I tried to forget when I moved to my new life in New York. But Blue Bell had been a nick-of-time vehicle find, and all that farm-driving probably prepared me for getting around here in rural Maine.

Craig, the *lobstah* guy, as Frannie liked to call him, had been more than kind when he agreed to sell old Blue Bell to me for a reasonable price. He'd used his bicycle until the weather turned cold, and he replaced his trusty bike with a superior cold-weather vehicle. I hadn't heard what kind.

I smiled as I approached the bend in the road that signaled the last turn before entering the official city limits of Misty Meadows. First stop: Hannaford's. After grabbing a few grocery items, I drove up to the bakery. The pet store was within walking distance, so I grabbed a few lovely toys for Sir Bogart before stepping under the striped awning and into the heavenly aromas of my best friend's bakeshop.

Frannie's disheveled head of curly red locks popped up from behind the counter and she yawned loudly before offering a greeting. "Sydney. Boy, are you a sight for sore eyes."

Chuckling, I pointed toward the table by the

window, and she nodded. A few minutes later, she joined me with two cups of coffee and two caramel-apple cupcakes. She placed one in front of me. "'Bout ready to try something new off the menu?"

I pulled the cupcake close and took an appreciative sniff. "You may find it hard to believe, but I honestly never get tired of eating these. Maybe it reminds me of my first day in town, or the fact that I'm lucky enough to have a friend like you, but that luscious caramel filling, the light crumb of the cupcake with bits of cooked apple, and then the pièce de résistance of the cinnamon buttercream . . . It's heaven."

Frannie laughed, despite her full mouth, and pointed to the name of the bakery painted on the window. Heaven Can Bake.

Taking a bite, I took the time to savor the apple and caramel, then I dabbed the corners of my mouth with a napkin. "You chose a genius name. And that's coming from someone who worked in the marketing business. The right name makes all the difference." Smiling, I scooped up my coffee.

She swiped a few crumbs into her hand and dropped them on a napkin. "Well, I know you had to put the kibosh on the tours after the murder and the bad publicity, so what are you and the three ghostly musketeers cooking up now?"

The great thing about having a best friend was being able to tell her everything. Frannie was in the know about all the mysterious and ethereal happenings at the manor. Not once had she called the sheriff in to tell me I was crazy. Well, maybe she did when we went through those time loops over and over, but I couldn't fault her for that one.

"Funny you should mention it," I said. "I was chatting with Sir Bogart this morning, and he suggested we take an inventory of everything in the mansion and see if there are some antiques worth selling."

Frannie nodded, and her expression turned thoughtful. "Would you use that auction house again? The one in New York that sold the rare wine for you?"

"I don't think so. There's probably not anything that valuable. Even if there is, I can get a website up and post enough enticing photos to get a good crowd to show up for a limited time event. If we make it super exclusive, and allow a day or two of previewing, and then let people submit bids on the high-end items, that should draw enough of a crowd to boost the sales of the smaller, less one-of-a-kind stuff."

Frannie set down her mug of coffee and curled her hands around its warmth. "You'll save on the auction house fee that way."

"That's my intent. I might be able to heat the manor for the winter, depending on how much cash I can get into my pockets."

"So you've totally got it under control. I should've known. Let me know if you need any baked goods on sale day."

I grinned. "Always. Nothing smells so good as fresh cookies in the oven. Maybe it'll inspire buyers to bid. Though, maybe this time you should cook them." I had burned them last time I tried to fill the air with the aroma of freshly baked goods. They'd all gone in the trash, and Sir Bogart tail-twitched his way through the house. Velma was much better at cooking and baking than I had ever been.

Her eyes widened, and she leaned toward me. "Oh, speaking of burning, have you heard about the Williams estate?"

At the mention of the estate of my recently deceased neighbor, my gossip antennas became fully engaged. "No . . ." I scowled, not recalling any giant plumes of smoke. "Did it burn down?"

"Oh, no, it just made me think about the burned-out chicken house between the properties. You know, burned in the boundary disputes."

The Williams and the Blodfyss ancestors had squabbled over the boundary line between them for many years. My recently deceased neighbor had been no exception after I moved into Moonlight Manor.

"Last I knew, the place was condemned," I offered, uncertain what the latest development might be.

She nodded vigorously. "Well, apparently it was. But it sounds like there's some big money from the Big Apple greasing a lot of palms. If they get a few things overturned and some permits are approved, you could have a brand-new next-door neighbor."

I shrugged. "I'm not worried. At least the property lines are settled, and no one could be worse than Gladys. God rest her and everything, but I don't think she'll be missed."

We shared a wicked chuckle, and Frannie agreed. "You know me. I try to see the best in everyone, but that woman was a real piece of work."

I leaned forward. "Do you have any information about the buyer? Like a name, marital status, or possible pets?"

Frannie arched an eyebrow, and her brown eyes twinkled. "What's this? Is Sydney Coleman inquiring about a potentially eligible bachelor? I thought you'd sworn off men."

My cheeks warmed. I had to pull off my stocking hat, exposing my swirly bed head of coffee-brown hair to let some heat escape. "Don't be silly. I was just asking. It was an innocent question. I'm not putting myself on the market or anything like that. I'm perfectly happy managing my own venture, and not having anyone to answer to."

She nodded, but her smug grin said she didn't believe a word I'd uttered.

They said time heals all wounds, and I supposed being dumped by Lucas Aconite was no exception. In fact, in the ensuing months since that fateful day, I'd realized the entire situation was more of a mental construct than a reality. Time and distance had given me a perspective I'd lacked when I was neck deep in the citified busy-ness.

Drumming my fingers on the table, I considered how long I'd been at my favorite place in town. "Listen, I better get back. Sir Bogart needs his new toys, and we'll have to get started on the inventory. I grabbed a couple of steaks and a salad kit. You're welcome to come out for supper if you don't have any special baking orders tonight."

"That sounds great. Maybe I can help with the

antique inventory. I think there are still a ton of rooms I haven't seen, and I'm handy with a clipboard and a pen. Who knows what we might find? It's like an exciting scavenger hunt right in your own home." She practically thrummed with excitement.

I stood and drained the remainder of my coffee. "Oh, I like that line. I might use it in some of the marketing copy. Anyway, I have to get back. Have a wonderful day, and we'll shoot for supper at 6:30?"

Frannie glanced toward the pastry case, tapped her bottom lip, and wiggled her shoulders back and forth. "That should be perfect. It's supposed to snow today, and if it really starts coming down, I might close early and head out your way sooner. Either way, 6:30 sounds great for food."

"Perfect. See you then." I tucked my coat around me and made my way toward the exit.

"See you when I see you." She smiled and waved as I hurried through the icy winds toward the vehicle.

While I drove back to the manor, I studied the sky. Frannie could be right. The clouds hung low, and their deep-gray color hinted at the hefty surprise they may be carrying.

My driving skills were all right, but I wasn't interested in testing them in nor'easter blizzard conditions. Besides, I couldn't afford to purchase a replacement car with cash, and Blue Bell had been a lucky find. Why risk it?

Yet concern about my food stores gripped me, and I carefully made a U-turn. Maybe I should stock up on some essentials. If I got snowed in, I would have plenty of room for Frannie to stay, but I definitely didn't have enough food.

Time to make a beeline back to the grocery store. This time I stocked up on canned goods, paper products, bottled water, batteries, matches, and loads of snacks. I even grabbed a bag of old-fashioned popcorn kernels. If the power went out, microwave popcorn would be useless, but this stuff . . .

I wasn't sure I possessed the skill to pop corn over an open fire in my fireplace, but it could definitely provide entertainment for Frannie and me.

3

It thrilled Velma when I returned home with so many bags of supplies.

She clasped her phantom hands in front of her chest and peered into the paper sacks. "Reminds me of the ol' days, miss. We used to get us a huge delivery every Tuesday. Mistress de Haviland loved to entertain. All sorts of things used to come in that delivery . . . food . . . decorations. It was near like Christmas every week."

I grinned at my manor companion. "You know, I'd love to entertain too, Velma. Maybe if this new venture—selling antiques—pays off, we can get back to the kind of parties Moonlight Manor deserves."

Her ghostly aura glowed, and she beamed with

pride. "Ah, that'd be grand, miss. It'd be right lovely to fill the rooms with life again."

I drew three cans from the sacks and turned around to put them away, but Velma swooped in and took them from me. She placed them on the floor beside the bags, humming an ethereal tune I didn't recognize.

When I approached to help, she waved me away and continued rifling through the bags. "Let me, miss."

I didn't argue with the cook. Instead, I moved to the sink and began rinsing dishes. "In the meantime, Frannie is coming out for a sleepover."

Velma paused in her unpacking of the canned goods. "That why you got so much grub?"

I had to laugh. When Frannie and I got together, there generally was an overconsumption of treats, and Velma's reasoning hit my funny bone. "No. They're predicting a big storm. It could blow over, but I wanted to be prepared. If we're snowed in, we'll need something to eat."

"That's wise, miss." Velma continued putting the groceries in the larder under the stairs.

I leaned against the cabinets while Velma's hustle and bustle brought back memories of my childhood in a farmhouse. "We got snowed in once when I was a kid. I grew up on a pig farm in Iowa, and we always had a root cellar full of staples. Plus, my mom canned vegetables, so there was never a concern that we would run out of food. However, being snowed in with two fiendish brothers had its downside, especially since we were stuck there for two weeks."

Out of the blue, Velma stopped her activity and sobbed.

"What's wrong? Is it a spirit thing?" I frowned as I stared at her.

She tipped her face toward me, met my gaze, her chin quivered, and then studied the floor again. "Beggin' your pardon, miss. It's been such a very long time since I seen my family. I had two young sons of my own."

"Oh, Velma." I hurried to her, hoping to comfort her, and reached to grasp her upper arm, but my fingers passed through her. If only I could comfort my friend in a real way. "I'm sure your husband kept your memory alive. I bet those boys didn't want for anything."

She sniffled and wiped at her nose with the corner of her apron. "My Henry was a good man. He worked at the Blodfyss shipyard. Twelve-hour shifts.

One break a day. But it never stopped him. No, sir. That man were as strong as an ox."

Nodding as I listened to Velma's story, this new piece of information caught my attention. "The Blodfyss family had a shipping business?"

She crossed her arms in front of herself. "That's right, miss. The father, Edward, built big ol' wooden ships in the old country. When he came here, he were already quite wealthy. He went and bought this plot of land, and he were the first to build steel ships in his yard. The Blodfyss ships was the best in the new world—according to Mistress de Haviland. They fetched a handsome price; I tell you. And the family were well cared for. They always says that man led a charmed life."

"Wow. I wish I could've met him." I wagged my eyebrows at her. "Was he handsome and powerful, or more hideous and frightening?"

She dusted off her hands as though she'd been baking and motioned for me to follow. "Come see for yourself, miss."

Velma led me to the gallery of portraits in the upstairs sitting room. "That large one in the center, above the fireplace, that'd be him."

The man cut a dashing figure. His wild raven

locks had been captured with loving detail by the artist. Edward Blodfyss looked dapper in his deep-blue tailcoat, burgundy cut-velvet patterned vest, and blue silk cravat. He wore a military style belt, which looked out of place, but it displayed a fancy piece of weaponry at his side. "That's quite a sword."

Velma nodded, but a different voice answered. Apparently, Sir Bogart had slipped into the room behind us during the viewing. "That would be the heirloom dagger of the Blodfyss family, mistress. It is no sword. Difference being, the blade is barely a tick longer than Master Blodfyss's elbow to fingertip length. That still places the implement in the category of dagger. Some would refer to it as a short sword, but I hardly think that would be appropriate." He then leapt onto an overstuffed settee and lounged languorously.

The short history lesson about blades interested me, and I couldn't help wondering what all the treasure-trove of a mansion might hold. "I stand corrected, Bogey. Whatever you call it, it's impressive. Do you think it's still here at the manor? Maybe in the attic?"

Sir Bogart's ears twitched, and he tilted his head. "Would you actually consider selling the item, mistress?"

I shrugged. "Maybe. I don't have any attachment to it. And there are no living descendants of the Blodfyss clan. If it would fetch us a good price, we can use the income."

A deep sadness drifted over the feline's apparition. His glow dimmed, and he sighed with decades of pain. His reply had little to do with the dagger. "I suppose you are right. Although, I doubt we will be able to locate the dagger. The Golden age of Master Blodfyss and his line has passed. Perhaps Moonlight Manor has already seen its best days."

My eyebrows lowered as I processed his dismissive, nearly pessimistic words. "Hey, I kind of take offense to that. I'm doing the best I can to keep this place afloat. But I'm no heiress to a shipping fortune."

At the mention of the family business, Sir Bogart seemed re-energized. "Did Velma mention their origins?"

"Yeah. She said Edward built ships back in England, and came to this country already a wealthy man."

Our feline overlord shook his head and his tail flicked with irritation. "Not exactly. Sir Edward Blodfyss was knighted by Queen Victoria for his outstanding contribution to shipbuilding for the royal navy. Had he stayed in England his life would have had only one path. He risked everything to come to the New World. His family had grown weary of class wars and religious oppression in the British Isles. Sir Blodfyss sold his business, his landholdings and abandoned his title. He and his family set sail for the New World aboard one of his own ships. It was a perilous journey, and several of his crew died at sea. The family arrived intact, but his wife had contracted typhoid on the voyage, and died shortly after their arrival. Edward was heartbroken. He had many an interested family attempting arrangements in the New World, and if truth be told, he allowed himself a fling or two, but he never remarried. He raised his five sons and two daughters on his own."

Velma was loath to interrupt Sir Bogart's heartfelt recitation, but she did cough.

The majestic cat turned toward the sound and seemed almost to frown. "My apologies, cook. Master Blodfyss had the assistance of a great many servants. It was remiss of me to neglect their mention." He briefly cleared his throat before finishing his tale. "Regardless, one of his sons died of scarlet fever before the age of ten, and another was badly injured in a dressage accident. He was never the same. The three remaining sons took up the business with the shipyard, but the youngest had an eye to the future.

He saw the true money would be in contracting to move goods back and forth across the vast ocean. The elder sister married well and her husband also joined the shipping business. Through careful planning and judicious contractual arrangements, eventually, Blodfyss ship building became the Blodfyss shipping industry. Sadly, the youngest sister, who married for love, died in childbirth."

As Sir Bogart told the tale of the family who built this magnificent manor, my heart filled with pride. "What about the grimoire? Before, you told me it was the Blodfyss sisters', and there were three. But it sounds like there were only two, and one passed."

The ghostly feline paused, and his eyes twinkled. "You are an apt student, mistress. The three brothers all married sisters from the same family. On a duck hunting expedition, they discovered the trio of beautiful, learned women living alone on the small island of Ilseboro. Legend has it that the brothers were enthralled by the three sisters and wed them within the month. The sons brought their new brides to the manor and lived out their days under the same roof. It was after the arrival of the sisters that the rumors of Blodfyss witches began to swirl."

"Fascinating. I love this place even more, now that I know a little more of its history." I shook my head. What were the odds all three brothers would meet three sisters and marry them? It made for an interesting snippet of ancestral narrative. Nevertheless, I had more immediate concerns. "I better get to work on the website for the estate sale. Thanks for the history lesson, Bogey."

He trotted toward the corner, curled up under a footstool, and squeezed his eyes closed.

It would definitely be enjoyable to spend the rest of the day building a website that would honor this family and their fabulous legacy. I may have to sell off their belongings to keep my head above water, but I wouldn't do it without paying proper tribute to this amazing bloodline.

Now that I understood the more personal side of the history of this grand estate, I wasn't clear about what items I would feel comfortable selling. It would take some study and meeting with the other three residents of the place before choosing what went and what stayed. But perhaps some of the portraiture could also be auctioned or donated.

Since His Felineness had such a grasp on historic events related to the family who once owned the mansion I now lived in, I shared some of my ideas. "Maybe we could donate the painting of Edward to the Maritime Museum. I'm not sure anyone will know any of the other folks in these paintings, but he seems to have played a large part in the history of shipping in the area."

Sir Bogart stood up, moaned mournfully as he stretched, and then paced along the walls of portraits. "I regret some of the names of those in these portraits have been lost, even to my acute memory."

"That's all right. Some buyers might be interested in the paintings for their historic value, but I'm afraid most will buy them simply for the frames."

Velma gasped dramatically, and Sir Bogart hung his head in shame. His voice was barely a whisper when he spoke. "May I ask that we keep the portrait of my mistress?"

"Of course. After solving her murder, I feel as though I knew Beatrix. I could never sell her painting. Besides, I'm not sure which we'll keep and which will go. It was simply an idea to go along with our auction." I considered the cat. "But I could never let Beatrix's portrait leave the manor."

He sighed with relief and vanished from my sight.

I turned to the cook. "Thanks for showing me that painting, Velma. I'm going to get to work on putting together the marketing materials for the estate sale. Would it be possible for you and Norman to start making a list of items for the sale? Maybe starting in the ballroom?"

She nodded, but made no verbal reply. Though, her expression remained wan.

I paused on the threshold of the portrait gallery. "Is something wrong?"

"There were some things I'd hoped you'd keep, miss."

I hoped my warm smile would soothe any concern Velma held. "Of course. Sorry, I forgot to mention that. Sir Bogart and I discussed that there would certainly be items that would have meaning for the three of you. We can move those things into one of the rooms we'll keep closed off during the event. Just put things on the list that we are all willing to part with. Okay?"

At first, she didn't answer.

"I know you'll be attached to things that are different than what Sir Bogart has a fondness for. And Norman will be different again." Since I hadn't lived at the manor in its heyday and I didn't know the inhabitants personally, I would care the least about which items we sold and which we kept. "Put the items on the list that we can all agree on."

"Thank you, miss." She curtsied and vanished.

While the cook and the butler worked on the

inventory, I needed to do some additional research on the family history, and create the eye-catching graphics and taglines that would draw people in from up and down the eastern seaboard. So I retrieved my laptop and got started on the project I hoped would save Moonlight Manor.

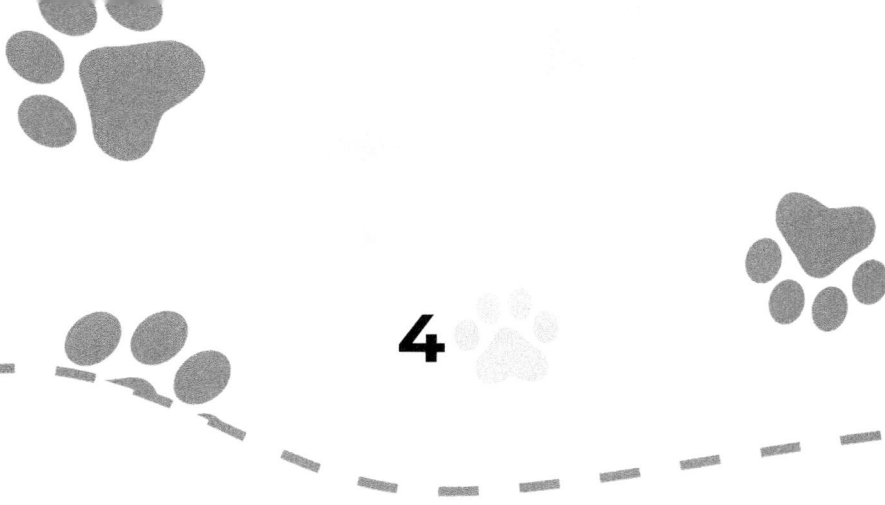

4

By the time Frannie arrived, I had uncovered enough information about the Blodfyss shipping company to create my own miniseries. They had been an active family throughout their lifespans. When the gong doorbell interrupted, I hurried from the warm kitchen where I'd been working to the grand foyer to let my friend inside.

One look at the pink box in my friend's hands and I was all smiles. "I grabbed a bunch of stuff at the grocery store today. But I'm way more interested to know what you brought."

She grinned as she stepped inside and tucked a loose strand of red hair behind her ear. "I brought four bacon and onion mini quiches, two caramel-apple cupcakes, and an undisclosed number of macarons."

I feigned a swoon. "My hero."

We both giggled as we walked to the kitchen to add her offerings to the supplies.

"Let me show you what I've been putting together for the estate sale." I opened my sleeping laptop and Frannie gazed over my shoulder as I scrolled through the graphics and rough marketing copy.

"That's all fantastic, Syd. Where did you get all this information? I hadn't heard this much around town. I'm not even sure Augusta Adams knows this much."

My mouth twisted at the mention of the local artisan and history keeper. She knew most of the town lore. "Well, Sir Bogart gave me the bones of their story, and after a few hours of research on the internet, I filled in the gaps. I think we could actually make some money with this sale."

She winked. "Well, Augusta is too old school to use the internet. Not to mention too stubborn about 'new-fangled ways.' "

I laughed and scrolled through the page once more. "I'll be selling some of the portraits as well. Though, I have mixed feelings about it. I don't know the people in them, but my roommates did."

She nodded her agreement and pointed to the photo I'd taken of Edward Blodfyss's portrait. "He is quite a looker. Was there a painting of his wife?"

"No, she contracted typhoid on the voyage from England. I didn't want to put any of the downer stuff in the story. I don't want people thinking anything might be cursed."

Frannie laughed loudly and nodded. "Good idea. You've already had your share of bad press and curses. Like that time loop."

I shuddered. "No kidding."

"So much better to stick to the positive things you can highlight on the family tree, and not draw any attention to the root rot."

We both chuckled, and I closed my laptop. "So, what are we doing at our slumber party? Telling ghost stories and brushing each other's hair?"

Frannie punched me playfully on the shoulder. "It's not that much of a stretch to tell ghost stories when you live with actual ghosts. And I don't think either of us has much interest in brushing our natural curls into frizz."

Shrugging my shoulders, I yawned as I attempted to conjure up other ideas.

"No yawning. It's a slumber party. We're supposed

to stay up super late. I can't have you yawning already, young lady."

I bit back another yawn and hoped Frannie wouldn't notice it. "That's fair. About the only thing I'm really good at is flat-ironing the curls *out* of my hair. Any interest?"

She smiled and shook her head. "No thanks. I promised myself I'd never touch one of those torture devices as long as I lived. I mean, after the years of horror I endured in New York. Once I left the corporate life behind, I smashed my flatiron with a hammer. I have no regrets."

Her courage and honesty always warmed my heart. Some days, New York felt like it had been a minute ago and other days it felt like it had been a lifetime ago. But Frannie understood me; she got me. She had her own similar tale of freedom.

I was starting to feel true happiness after leaving the New York hustle and bustle behind, but every once in a while when I caught sight of my natural curls going wild in some reflective surface, I longed for the sleek and shiny hair of my past. Though, I sure couldn't afford the top-notch salon visits on my limited budget.

I waved my hand between us. "Well, we can binge-watch something, maybe play a board game—"

Frannie leaned toward me and whispered. "What about a treasure hunt?"

"What do you mean?" I froze. Treasure hunt?

"I don't know. Let's search through the mansion, and try to find that one amazing treasure that will fetch a ridiculous price at your estate sale." She sort of danced on her toes, giving away how excited she was about the idea of a treasure hunt in Moonlight Manor.

I couldn't stop my grin. My friend hadn't spent as much time here as I had, and she hadn't been in all the closets and shelves, so I couldn't fault her desire to explore.

A magnificent image flashed to mind. "You know what? That's actually a great idea. Let me show you something." I led her to the portrait gallery and pointed to the sapphire and diamond encrusted sheath on the dagger in Edward's belt. "Let's try to find this."

She let out a low whistle, nodded, and flashed her eyebrows. "That is faaaaaan-cy. Do you think it's still here?"

"Bogey doesn't believe it's here."

"But what do you believe?"

Shrugging, I raised my hands in a gesture meant to encompass the whole of the mansion. "With the whole manor to hide it, it's absolutely a possibility. There are rooms I haven't even been in. Who knows, we might find another secret passage while we're at it."

Frannie rubbed her hands together in anticipation. "Now it's a slumber party."

5

The great thing about pretty much any activity involving Frannie was the way she added lightness and humor. Enthusiasm flowed out of her and turned everything cheerful. She swiped a scrap of newspaper, probably leftover from when I moved in, and folded it into a triangle-shaped hat. Then she plunked it on her head. It rested on top of her bright red curls.

She winked. "Like my hat?"

"It certainly makes you look the part of an intrepid seeker of things."

"I told you. *Now* it's a slumber party." She spun in a slow circle. "Where should we search first?"

"I'm not sure, but we need provisions for the journey."

"I know what that means." She grinned and doffed her paper hat. "Wine cellar."

We opened a bottle of wine from the secret cellar beneath the ballroom and poured two stemless glasses quite full, before beginning our methodical search—which started on the ground floor. We were like two grand explorers embarking on the adventure that would define their lifetime.

We agreed that every cabinet, wardrobe, bureau, highboy, and hutch would be thoroughly searched. The ballroom seemed a great place to start. There was hardly any furniture, and we kept cracking each other up, whispering inappropriate jokes in the acoustically perfect space.

I had a distant middle school memory of learning about such a spot in the U.S. Capitol building in Washington, D.C. There seemed to be a similar "whispering gallery" location in the ballroom. As I stood and whispered various hilarious quips for Frannie's benefit, I could easily imagine powerful men and women from the past discovering this fantastic location. Perhaps gaining shrewd insights through the softly spoken gossip from all sections of the bustling ballroom. All while wearing the multi-layered finery that defined the times.

Frannie called out from across the room. "Hey, check out what I found in this piano bench."

I couldn't believe our luck. What if she'd found the dagger in the first room we searched? Could it have been in the piano bench this whole time? I ran toward her with a childish thrill coursing through my chest.

However, when I arrived and saw nothing more than yellowed sheets of paper, my heart sank. "Shoot. I thought you found it."

She shrugged. "It's no dagger, but these compositions could fetch a pretty penny if you find the right music lover. Might be worth it to include in your sale."

I thumbed through the crinkled pages and shrugged. "I don't know anything about music. What makes you think they're valuable?"

Carefully, she shuffled through the papers again. "It looks like an opera in progress. Do you see that signature? William Grant Still? If that can be authenticated, this could be a draft composition from one of his great works. I'm telling you, the right collector would pay a fortune for something like this."

I scowled and pursed my lips. "Really?"

She nodded. "I'm sure of it."

"Fantastic. I'll let Velma and Norman know. It's

not a gorgeously ornate weapon, but they can add the composition to the official inventory."

We walked around the vast room, with its lovely domed ceiling, carefully searching the walls for any sign of a secret passage but came up empty-handed.

"What's next?" Frannie took a sip from the wine glass she'd carried with her.

"On to the billiard room," I said.

But there were no secret compartments in the billiard table, and nothing but chipped billiard balls in the sideboard. I had no idea why they would've saved the damaged spheres. Maybe they planned to have them polished or repaired. Honestly, I wasn't sure if that was even possible—just an uneducated guess.

Into the drawing room. This room was filled with fine furniture, and there were plenty of drawers and other compartments to search. Except, we found nothing out of the ordinary and no dagger. We already knew about the secret passage leading from the drawing room to the second-floor burgundy room, so we left the passage alone for the time being and continued to search the ground level. Once the ground level had been completed, we would address the secret passage and the next level. We moved across the foyer and into the library. Now this room would take some time. In fact, we both became so absorbed in the task that we set our half-full wine glasses down on the enormous desk.

"Up or down?" I asked, scanning the large room. So many hiding places.

"Up," Frannie said.

"Then I'll take down."

Frannie removed her newspaper hat and placed it in the waste bin, then she climbed the ladder and carefully began her search of the upper shelves. She ran her hands over each row of books, tilting various suspicious-looking titles to see if they triggered the opening of any hidden compartments or doors.

I searched the antique furniture. There were a multitude of drawers, and I located a secret compartment behind a drawer in the desk, but it was empty. Not to worry, I moved on to checking the lower shelves. Having completed my search of the main library, I moved into the portion beneath the second-floor study which jutted inside of the hexagonal tower.

When I reached the wall that would be immediately adjacent to the terrace outside the front entrance, I felt behind a section of volumes on the shelf, and my hand hit something unexpected. "Frannie. I've got something."

She shrieked, scurried down the ladder with surprising speed, and joined me. "Is it the dagger?"

Trembling, I took a breath in an attempt to calm myself. "No, but there's a strange piece of metal behind these books."

Her brown eyes sparkled with child-like wonder. "Tilt them back."

I gripped the wide tome and tilted it outward, just like I'd read about in so many of my favorite childhood books.

There was an audible click and both of us covered our mouths with our hands.

We stepped out of the way as a section of the built-in bookcase hinged toward us. Stale air with a hint of dusty disuse hit us firmly in our faces. For the hundredth time, I couldn't believe I'd had the good fortune to leave New York and end up owning Moonlight Manor.

Grabbing my phone from my back pocket, I hit the light. "You ready?"

She squealed with delight. "You know it."

I stepped into the narrow passage inside the thick wall and followed the stone stairs as they climbed upward. They were steep and seemed to turn at evenly spaced left angles. I stopped on the third section. "I think the steps are following the planes of the hexagonal tower. But it seems like we've passed the second floor. We have to be nearly to the third floor."

Frannie gripped my arm and whispered quietly. "Keep going. I know it's gonna be worth it."

Taking a shallow breath of the musty air, I continued upward. After two more turns, we were richly rewarded. Frannie and I stumbled into a hidden room in the cone top of the hexagonal tower. A hint of light bled in through windows, but the hidden room remained shadowed. Soon, it would be completely dark.

As I gazed around the space, I tried to make sense of its existence. "The butler's room on the third level must be smaller than it seems. That hidden stairway seems to wrap around it entirely. The walls must be super thick up there as well."

Frannie pointed to the floor, and I directed my phone light to where she pointed. "So we're above the butler's quarters?"

"Exactly. I thought the rest of the tower was simply decorative. I had no idea there was anything up here. The round tower on the opposite side of Moonlight Manor is open all the way up from the burgundy room clear up to the roof. Obviously, I made some false assumptions."

I pointed my light as Frannie searched the walls and eventually found a two button electrical switch. "Whoever updated the electric knew about the room up here."

"True." Could there be other hidden rooms in the mansion? It was turning into quite the character, ever surprised as we slowly coaxed the secrets out into the open.

"Ready?" she breathed.

I nodded. "Surely the wiring is still good up here."

"Here goes nothing," Frannie murmured.

When the soft, creamy light of the sconces illuminated the space, we gasped in unison.

"It's like a hidden apothecary." Shelves held bottles and bottles of liquid, powder, and herbs. The containers were made up of clear glass, brown glass, cobalt, and many more. Most were so dusty I couldn't clearly make out what they held. Some boasted dingy labels and others didn't. A dusty island sat in the middle of the room. Odd medical and scientific-looking instruments sat upon it, books filled shelves, and a clutch of small wooden drawers beckoned from the corner.

Every cell in my body was drenched in amazement. I shared a highly abbreviated version of the

Blodfyss brothers' adventures on Ilseboro, and their subsequent marriages to three mysterious sisters.

Frannie grinned and shook her head. "So you only heard the story today and found the secret room the same day. I don't think that's a coinkydink." She clapped her hands and made another excited exclamation. "Let's start on either side of the secret door and head in opposite directions. Who knows what we might uncover?"

I grinned like the Cheshire cat. "Sounds like a plan."

Giggling, we bolted toward the entrance to the secret room and each took a position on either side.

"Ready?" I asked, wagging my eyebrows at my companion in this adventure.

When Frannie nodded, we each took a dramatic step away. It felt almost like we were in the middle of pacing off a duel in a movie. We were each about halfway around our sides of the room when—

"Supper is served, madam."

The two human occupants of the secret apothecary screamed.

"Norman. You scared the daylights out of us." My chest heaved, and I swallowed convulsively to wet my now-dry throat.

"My apologies, madam. I had been searching the

manor for you. I was not aware you had access to this room."

Frannie's finger danced at the base of her throat. "Does he always pop up like that?"

"Sometimes. But he has to work to make himself visible to anyone other than me."

She tilted her head. "Good to know."

Turning, I eyed the butler suspiciously. "Norman, I'm the mistress of this manor. I have access to all the rooms. I can't believe you were holding out on me. Have you always known of this room?"

He gripped his hands behind him and gave a curt bow. "Again, my apologies, madam. I had hoped this room would remain forgotten. The Blodfyss sisters were capable of great good, but in their later years, the stories of their acts become twisted with jealousy and revenge. It may not be my place to decide, but I felt their secrets best left buried. At least as long as these secrets wished to remain hidden." He added the last almost as an afterthought.

His words seemed sincere, but a sudden thought derailed my trust. "If *this* was their secret room? How did their precious grimoire get into the attic?"

The specter did not reply.

6

He lacked an answer. In the months I'd been in Moonlight Manor, I'd never had a reason to doubt Norman. Yet, now, a feeling of suspicion and mistrust that I had never experienced when dealing with Norman washed over me.

I stepped toward Frannie and gripped her elbow, hoping to borrow some of her courage. "Norman, how did the Blodfyss grimoire get into the attic?"

His image flickered, and I feared he planned to disapparate. I took a step toward him. "Norman, as mistress of the manor, I must insist that you answer me."

Somehow, my assertion of rank compelled him.

His form snapped back to its previous strength, and he inclined his head. "Mistress de Haviland was fond of using an occasional spell to her own benefit. Sir Bogart warned her many times about the tax one must pay when magic is used selfishly, but she refused to heed his warnings."

"So, Beatrix used magic to gain her status and acclaim?" Although magic hadn't allowed Beatrix to attain the level of fame she wished, perhaps it had bolstered her. I met Frannie's gaze, but my friend didn't add anything. She was probably still too overwhelmed by the existence of a hidden apothecary and my conversation with the ghost butler, floating smack-dab in the middle of it. Though, Frannie probably couldn't see him. Most guests couldn't see my phantom roomies. I only could because I had declared myself the mistress of the manor.

Norman's hands came around to the front, and he wrung them several times before answering. "I do not wish to defame my former mistress. It is not as though she relied heavily on the tome. It was an occasional entertainment."

"Why didn't you return the book to this room? It was in the attic when I found it."

"I believed hiding it in the attic would be sufficient. None of the previous visitors ever stayed long enough to give us concern, and most do not spend time in the attic of a haunted house. When we heard you intended to buy the home, we had little time to prepare. Perhaps I wasn't thinking clearly, madam."

I took a breath as the feeling of distrust dissipated slightly. "Norman, I'm upset that you kept this room from me, but I believe you thought it was in my best interest."

He bowed deeply. "I truly did, madam."

"Now that we've discovered it," I grinned at the still-silent Frannie, "would you mind sharing your knowledge of the space in hopes of preventing us from injury, or possibly misuse of these powerful substances?" No use allowing his erudition to go to waste.

"Of course. However, Sir Bogart retains far more knowledge than I. Perhaps you may refer to him after the initial tour is completed."

Perhaps this was Norman's respectful way of asking me to not ask him anything else after today. I would probably oblige him, but for now I had to know what he knew. "As you wish. Please continue," I said, not quite enjoying how "mistress-y" I sounded in my own ears. Norman didn't seem to mind at all, and Frannie barely batted an eye.

"Yes, mistress," Norman intoned. He slowly walked around, gesturing to specific shelves, tables, instruments, and books. He explained the basic principles of the herbs, and indicated books that would have additional details on the names that were unfamiliar to him. "As you can see, they labeled everything with the proper Latin names. Laypersons often confuse similar colors or shapes of leaves. By using the correct Latin names, the sisters took extreme care that their potions and hex bags would contain the proper elements."

I reached toward a jar labeled *Aconitum napellus*, and mumbled, "Aconite?"

Norman whooshed toward me and placed a gentle hand on mine. "That is deadly, madam."

"What does it mean, ay-cone-item nay-plus?" I struggled with the strange words, and the sisters' calligraphy.

Norman ignored my mispronunciation and uttered the proper Latin name as it appeared on the label. "*Aconitum napellus*. It is commonly known as Wolf's Bane, mistress. It may paralyze the nerves, lower blood pressure, and gradually stop the heart."

I let his voice drift far away, as memories of Lucas Aconite bumped around in my head. There was a sudden sense of clarity about the way he had slowly numbed me to my true self and eventually broken my heart. "I guess I shouldn't be surprised."

Frannie moved toward me. "I hate to interrupt. This is all fascinating, but how come I can see and hear Norman this time?" She sounded breathless, and I realized maybe she hadn't spoken at all because the shock of Norman's appearance had taken her voice.

"So you can see him and hear him this time?" I echoed.

She nodded, trembling. "Yeah."

It wasn't until she had asked her question out loud that I realized she'd been following along with Norman for the first time since she'd been a visitor at the manor. "Yeah, I thought I was the only one who could hear you as you. How are you doing this?"

Velma could whisper in ears and echoey scream from a distance, and she'd used those skills during the haunted tours, but that wasn't the same as the conversation I was now having with Norman. This had to be somewhat unsettling for unflappable Frannie.

Norman nodded to the space around us. "It is the work of this room, madam. The sisters' implements are steeped in magic. And the wards they placed on this room require that all entities who enter reveal themselves fully."

"How interesting." Frannie moved toward Norman. She didn't offer her hand to the ghost, but she grinned up at him. "I saw you faintly during the haunted mansion tours. But I always wondered what you sounded like. Pleased to meet you."

Norman clasped his hands behind him and offered a shallow bow. He almost beamed at Frannie, and I had to think it was nice for him to meet someone besides his mistress after all these years. "It is a pleasure to meet you, Miss Clark."

Scanning the room, I noted the shelves and the bins. "Norman, we're searching for the dagger. Do you have any knowledge of its whereabouts?"

"I do not, madam. However, I believe your best luck will be found in this room. If there was an item to be coveted, or perhaps rumored to be charmed, the sisters would have acquired it and kept it where only their eager hands might wield it."

Frannie smiled and patted me conspiratorially on the back. "That's encouraging. Don't you think, Syd?"

"Definitely. Let's head downstairs and refuel. I'd say we have at least two or three more hours' worth of searching in this convoluted room after supper."

She nodded. "Sure thing."

Norman vanished through the wall, and we returned through the sharply angled secret passage.

Twisting our way down to the library as though we had walked into an Escher painting.

Back on the ground floor, I took a deep breath of fresh air. "Just when I thought things couldn't get any stranger."

She shook her head and shrugged. "I know, right? I can't wait to get back up there. Some of those odd instruments must be worth a fortune. The delicate glass lenses and finely wrought brass knobs . . . It's unlikely that many others would have survived from that era."

Velma had prepared a delicious winter stew of hardy chunks of ham, root vegetables, and a fresh note of parsley. She'd also baked a lovely loaf of soda bread, which impressed even Frannie. "Velma, I can't see you, so I don't know if you're here, but this bread is amazing. I'd love to get the recipe."

Velma phased through the wall from the larder, grinning from ear to ear. "Tell Miss Frannie I'd be happy to oblige." I passed along the message.

Frannie thanked the cook, and Velma curtsied. I relayed it all.

Without further ado, we tucked into our delicious supper and sopped up every bit of the tasty gravy with chunks of still-warm bread.

As we ate, Frannie over-dramatized her mental

confusion over the ethereal Norman, and we laughed over the re-telling of the butler's appearance in the hidden room. While Frannie had been shocked speechless, she was still as cool as a cucumber. Though, exploring secret rooms was entirely less frightening with good friends in tow.

"You know, I think most people would have run out of here screaming if they'd met Norman in a hidden room."

"It's not like I didn't know he existed. But, on that note, most owners would have immediately put Moonlight Manor up for sale the first time a trio of specters demanded she find out who murdered their previous mistress."

"Touché."

Finally, with our resolve and our bodies freshly fortified, we headed back to the library and the secret entrance.

"Ah ha." Frannie hustled over to the desk and lifted her wine from before. "Let's have a toast to a successful search."

Giggling, I lifted my glass and lightly clinked it against hers. "To the dagger."

She echoed my sentiment, and we downed the remainder of our wine.

Back in the warmly lit apothecary, our search continued.

However, our efforts were frequently interrupted with fascinating finds that had to be shared, and added to the growing list on my notes app. So many interesting gadgets gathered dust in the hidden location above the butler's quarters.

For some reason, we could not access the internet from this room, and I had a sneaking suspicion that the wards placed by the sisters did more than reveal visiting entities. Perhaps this place was truly hidden from prying eyes of all frequencies. Though, if this were true, how had we been allowed to find it?

By the time we finished the six floor-to-ceiling panels of books, cupboards, and drawers, we were exhausted and losing faith. Hours had gone by. The moon had risen to roughly forty-five degrees above the horizon and glowed through the pointed-arched windows.

Suddenly, Frannie yelped and pointed. I turned to follow the trajectory of her finger and my voice caught in my throat. The moonlight had hit one of the fine instruments on the center island, and its refraction cast an image on a narrow panel located between two sections of the bookcase. In any other light, that panel would have remained invisible, hidden by the shadows of the shelves surrounding it.

Finally, loosening my vocal cords, I whispered, "Are you seeing what I'm seeing?"

Frannie nodded in silence.

7

"That is known as a moon mark."

Thanks to the revelatory powers of the secret room, Frannie and I simultaneously jumped out of our skin. We clutched each other in fright as the majestic ghost of Sir Bogart emerged from the shadows, looking more regal than ever before.

"How did you find us? How do you know what that is? Why did it get so dark in here?" The questions tumbled out of me in rapid-fire fashion.

Beside me, Frannie remained quiet.

The lordly feline sat calmly on the floor and curled his velvet rope of a tail around his large paws. "To your first query, Norman informed me of your recent discovery of the sisters' secret workshop. To your second, I have had decades to study the history of Moonlight Manor, and countless hours to explore the powerful and sometimes deadly contents of this room. And to your final inquiry, the sisters were skilled in many areas beyond magic. It was Vernetta, who had a penchant for engineering and rigged the lighting to respond to moonlight."

"Respond *how*?" Perhaps we needed to duck before a beam of moonlight sprung some sort of trap. "Will it be dangerous?"

Frannie patted my arm as though she, too, was pleased with my question.

"You will experience the specifics shortly, but when the moon strikes this room with a certain brilliance, it automatically dampens the natural lighting. The sisters performed many works solely by the light of the moon, and it benefited them to perfect a system with lunar sensitivities. However, it was Arthetta who crafted the magic behind the moon marks. And young Rosetta developed different symbols for their clandestine purposes. Together, the sisters were able to hide objects of power in places where only they could recover them."

My gaze narrowed as I studied the feline. "But how do you know all this?"

"I have had many years since my mistress's death

to study the abilities of the three sisters, based on the works they've left behind."

Pointing to the glowing cross on the panel of wood, I gulped. "So that's not a crucifix?"

Bogey turned, tilted his head, and stared at the marking. "Ah, I see it now. No, mistress, this is no exorcism. I believe upon further examination you will deduce that the mark is that which you seek, as unrecommended as wielding it is."

His words were nothing more than a riddle, but Frannie gripped my arm and squeezed hard. "Syd, it's not a cross. It's a dagger."

I moved toward the glowing symbol and, as my hands brushed the wood panel, Sir Bogart uttered one of his cryptic warnings. "Before you grasp the Dagger of Desire, be sure your heart is pure."

"It's not Excalibur, Bogey. I'm not going to rule a kingdom or anything. The plan is to examine it, and decide whether it's an heirloom we keep, or an antique we sell. Simple enough, right?" Though, even as I discounted the warning, the grimoire came to mind. But a dagger was different, wasn't it? Of course it was.

I nodded once. "So I only need to make sure I don't go reading any more strange poems out loud. Got it."

He scoffed and vanished into the secret stone tunnel.

The moon mark flickered and disappeared, as the sconces bloomed with light.

Frannie had a hand pressed firmly to her chest. "This place is a heart attack a minute. I don't know how you do it."

I shrugged. "Me neither. Let's see if we can figure out how to open this panel."

There was no obvious handle on the thin piece of wood. We tried tipping various books on either side of the wooden slat, and eventually resorted to plain old prying. Nothing worked, and I wasn't about to call the trio of apparitions into the room. Sir Bogart wouldn't be back to help. Plus, I already knew how Norman felt about it, and Velma still hadn't even followed us up here. She probably wanted to be as far away from here as possible.

Finally, with a belabored grunt, Frannie thumped the panel in frustration and it popped right open. She chuckled. "I guess even a blind squirrel finds a nut every once in a while."

Laughing, I took a deep breath and reached into the dark recesses of the narrow compartment.

Frannie flinched as my hand went into the space, and I startled. When I turned toward her, she gave me a sheepish, apologetic look. "Sorry," she whispered. "Too many scary movies."

I shook my head and reached in as deeply as I could. There was a hard object wrapped in silk. My hand closed around it, and a thrill rushed through me. Had we found the dagger from the portrait?

I carefully extracted the piece, carried it to an open space on the island in the center of the room then lowered it gently. Barely able to breathe, I met Frannie's shining gaze over the found package. "Should we?"

"Open it, open it," she said. "It's what we came for."

"Let's do it together."

Slowly unwrapping several of the luxurious layers, we gasped when the sparkling diamonds of the hilt were revealed. "This is it. We found Edward's dagger."

There was a miniature scroll tucked into the folds of the material surrounding the blade. I extracted it and carefully unfurled the message.

"Beware. Whoever discovers this deadly poniard. My sisters and I were unable to alter its fate. It was with great sadness that we buried Reginald Williams after the unsavory incident. But a greater sorrow still when we three were forced to traverse space and time to thieve

Sir Edward's prized possession and place it beyond his reach for all eternity. Heed my warning. Lest you meet a similar fate."

Rosetta Blodfyss. And for my sisters beyond the veil.

Locking eyes with Frannie once more, I dropped the note and stepped away from the dagger, wringing my hands. At least the wind hadn't blown a chill through the room after I read the note, but this whole thing was definitely beginning to feel like the grimoire situation all over again.

Maybe Sir Bogart had been right. Though, we *did* find our way out of the other mess mostly unscathed.

"You know, Bogey mentioned Vernetta and Arthetta. They must have died before Rosetta wrote this note, and yet somehow helped her steal the knife. What if they were ghosts? Wow. This dagger sounds pretty dangerous. Maybe we should wrap it back up and forget we ever found the thing."

Frannie scoffed and shook her head. "Sydney, don't let this nineteenth century nonsense get to you. We both know that anything people didn't understand, they readily blamed on the paranormal. These sisters may have been considered educated—for their time—but science has come a long way since then. Whatever terrible power they thought the dagger possessed, the 'unsavory incident' was much more likely the result of a mental instability in their patriarch Edward Blodfyss."

I chewed my bottom lip as I studied the dagger on the island. Maybe she had a point. In general, what she said was true, and it was common knowledge that the shallow gene pools among the British and European nobility had led to more than one or two strange illnesses. For example, hemophilia was far more common amongst royalty than peasants. Perhaps the same was true of the Blodfyss family.

I lowered my hands. "Yeah. You're right. It's just being in this weird room and seeing the spooky moon mark that set me off. I'm certain it's just a dagger. It may have a gorgeous jewel-encrusted scabbard, but in the end, it's a simple knife." Not a grimoire.

"Exactly."

"Only one way to find out anyway."

Frannie pantomimed smoking a cigar and donned a terrible faux-German accent. "Sometimes a dagger is just a dagger, Sydney."

Our laughter echoed down the twisting secret passage as I carried the silk wrapped treasure back to the blue room. After all, my bedroom could benefit from the extra bling. I placed the dagger on my bedside table, its blade still wrapped in silk.

I'd already offered Frannie the adjoining amber

room, and now I unlocked the connecting door for her. I retrieved a selection of snacks from the kitchen while Frannie searched for Christmas-themed movies to help get us in the spirit.

The search had been a success, and now it was time to get down to the "party" portion of our sleepover.

8

Frannie must've slipped out at the break of dawn. I had a faint memory of some creaking floorboards, but nothing more. The light peeking around my heavy drapes seemed bleak. I slid them back and peered through the fractals of frost that crept across the window.

Everything was white as far as the eye could see. I wrapped my thick robe tightly, tied the sash, and walked to the French doors leading onto the terrace at the front of the manor.

The only break in the spotless blanket of snow draped over my estate came from the two determined tire tracks that forced their way toward the main road. *Go, Frannie. Feed the world. Or at least Misty Meadows.*

Now I understood why Frannie had a four-wheel-drive vehicle. Running a bakery was serious business. People relied on coffee and doughnuts like Wall Street relied on—crooks? Laughing at my own clever analogy, I headed toward the kitchen for a hot cup of coffee.

My sleepover guest had left heating instructions for the two remaining mini quiches, and I popped them into the oven to warm while I got busy making the java.

Breakfast was unusually quiet. No ghosts, no calls or texts, not even a breeze to ruffle the naturally flocked pine trees.

Before diving into another day of inventory, I returned to my room to take one more look at the fascinating vintage weapon. I hadn't yet decided if I would sell it or not. Perhaps a reexamination would help me make the final choice.

Placing the silk parcel on the blue duvet, I carefully unwrapped it, and scooped it up with the gentleness of a mother cradling a newborn babe. The diamonds were blindingly white, and the sapphires each held the radiance of a star in their centers. Turning the golden scabbard over in my hand, I drew the blade. It gleamed as though it had been freshly polished. As I moved toward the window to see if I could decipher the fine etching on the blade, the edge of shiny metal caught my reflection, and I smiled.

Your hair is the most gorgeous ebony hue.

I scowled. Normally, the voices in my head weren't complimenting me. Most people would say I was my own harshest critic. What a weird comment. Especially since it was in the second person. That was not how I would talk about myself.

I attempted to catch another glimpse of my reflection, but this time I heard a different praise, once again in the second person.

The golden flecks in your eyes are that of high-born status.

"Well, thank you, kind dagger." The voice wasn't my own, of that I was sure, but I could get used to being complimented all the time. No wonder Edward carried this thing on his belt. It was always nice to have a cheerleader in your corner.

Reluctantly returning the blade to the sheath, I received an additional message.

You are most clever and deserving of success.

"Thanks again." I loosely wrapped the silk around the dagger and placed it on the dressing table. It was becoming clear to me why Sir Bogart had referred to it as the Dagger of Desire. After hearing those positive things, I absolutely felt more desirable. It was basically a mental reminder to be kinder to myself. I thought it was fantastic. Maybe I wouldn't auction that off, after all. I made my way out of my room and to the top of the imperial staircase.

"Norman? Velma?" A moment later, the ghosts of the butler and the cook appeared in the grand entrance at the base of the staircase.

"Good morning. I'm going to inventory the attic today. I could use some help."

Norman bowed. "Of course, madam."

Velma offered a quick curtsy. "Yes, miss."

They popped up to the second floor, and I led the way to the spiral staircase that rose to the third level, past the portrait of Beatrix de Haviland, to the door with the cloudy robin's egg blue and mostly cobalt blue knob. Turning the glass handle on the narrow door, I opened it to reveal a steep staircase leading almost straight up. As I climbed toward the attic, the bleak light seeping through the round windows in the dormers offered barely sufficient illumination.

The ghosts had, of course, arrived ahead of me.

Once I stepped into the attic, I gestured to the contents. "Let's start over on the far side and work our way back toward the stairs. We should go through every crate and trunk. Some of the items may not be worth selling, and some may be headed straight to the trash bin, but there should be several things that we can add to the sale. We can reorganize while we're in here, and I'd like to know what all is up here anyway."

The helpers nodded, and we began the process. Before we made it even one third of the way across the clutter, my phone rang loudly and startled even the apparitions. I glanced at the screen and then at my helpers. "It's Mia Jones, the realtor. I better answer."

They both nodded, and I placed the phone against my ear. "Hello, Mia. What's up?"

As she spoke, my mood darkened. And when the call ended, I tossed the phone onto a nearby trunk and stepped back as though it might attack.

"Is something wrong, madam?" Norman floated to my side and awaited instruction.

"Everything is all right—for now. I think I better find Sir Bogart, and tell all of you the news at the same—"

"I am here, mistress. The sentimental part of me worried you may earmark my old implements of entertainment for the trash heap."

His silly love for his tattered toys eased a fraction

of my concern. "Like we agreed, if anybody feels strongly about keeping something, it stays. We're all in this together."

Nods of agreement circled the group.

"Now then, what was your news, mistress?" Sir Bogart leapt onto a green and black trunk with thick leather straps and waited with feigned interest. With the fate of his old play things secured, he didn't want to be here anymore.

Pointing to my phone, I inhaled sharply. "That was Mia Jones. She wanted to let me know that the sale went through on the old Williams estate. The buyer is Kenny Holt."

Bogey groomed his whiskers and gazed at me from the corner of his eye. "This name means nothing to us. Does it carry particular meaning for you?"

I groaned and sighed at the same time. "Kenny Holt runs the second largest agency in Manhattan. Holt Streak. We were always going up against them in bids for big accounts. He and my ex, Lucas, maintained some civility in public, but their rivalry was intense."

The aloof feline dropped to his side and cleaned his left front paw. "All alpha males battle for territory and attention. Nothing for you to concern yourself with, mistress."

"You don't understand, Bogey. One time Lucas had a thousand cases of champagne delivered to their office, just to keep them from arriving on time for a presentation. We got the business, and it was worth millions." The memory of Lucas's smug grin turned my stomach. "Kenny Holt swore he'd get even."

"Very well. I admit this fruitless battling may be beyond my understanding, but how can it possibly concern you, mistress?" Bogey casually closed his eyes.

"No idea. But this guy just bought the land right next door to me—in Maine. His enemy is my ex. It cannot be a coincidence. How would he even hear about a rundown, condemned place like that? And why? Why would he want it?"

Sir Bogart did not respond.

Norman stepped in. "Madam, I believe it is in your best interest to let sleeping dogs—"

Bogey hissed with all the rage of a truly vengeful spirit.

"Cool your canines, Bogey," I said, and he hissed again as though his life depended on it, and I hid a smile. Sir Bogart despised all mention of dogs in any form, including when referring to his fangs, but at least his ire had now returned to me.

Norman bowed slightly. "Begging your pardon, Sir Bogart. It was a poor choice of words." He turned to me. "What I meant to say, madam, was that we have plenty to keep us busy. There's little chance of Mr. Holt having reason to visit Moonlight Manor."

9

It was the last day of preparation before the estate sale preview. Most of the manor still had to be cleaned and freshened, and I also needed to affix small signs to the various rooms and areas that would be off-limits. I had flyers printed to explain how things would work and planned to hand them out as guests entered.

The first of my helpers to arrive were Cheryl and Joe Johnson. Cheryl and I had met previously, when she helped with the initial cleaning of Moonlight Manor. She was my realtor's sister-in-law, an odd person who really enjoyed snooping through other people's things. Apparently, she enjoyed it enough to work for free—which was fine by me. She'd mentioned her husband worked for Sheriff Allen, but we'd never had the pleasure of meeting.

I stood on the granite steps with my large mug of coffee and waved to the couple. "Hi Cheryl. This must be Joe."

The unassuming man ran a nervous hand through his brown hair before returning my greeting. As they passed by the fountain in the front yard, he gave an uncomfortable smile and nod.

Cheryl elbowed him. "Yes. He's excited to see the place. How is the setup going, Sydney?"

Cheryl was fond of wild hair colors, and her previous bright blue had been replaced with something I'd heard referred to as mermaid hair. There were greens, purples, and pinks streaked into the mix, but somehow it looked adorable on her.

"Oh, Cher, I love the new do." I shook my head. Only she could pull it off in a town this size.

"Thanks." She beamed and subsequently stared at me in silence. "Gosh, Sydney. Speaking of hair, I hardly recognized you. Is your hair naturally curly?"

When Cheryl first met me, I still reeked of all things New York City. "Yes. I used to straighten it. But it takes a lot of time, and it's kind of hard on your hair."

She tilted her head and nodded. "I think you look

fantastic. Much happier than when we first met. The curls are totally you."

I didn't want to get into all the ways Misty Meadows and Moonlight Manor were so much more me than New York City. So, instead, I said, "Why don't you guys come in and get a cup of coffee? As soon as Davis gets here, we'll start moving down the big pieces."

Joe took an odd step, caught his toe on something, and stumbled at the bottom of the stairs. As though she were psychic, Cheryl instantly caught his elbow. "Take it easy, Joseph Johnson. You're gonna be handling valuable items today. I expect you to be twice as careful as usual and at least half as clumsy."

Joe's cheeks blushed as he gazed at his wife with unconditional love. "I'll do my best, Cheryl."

She looked at me and chuckled. "He's lucky Davis will be on the other end of anything he's carrying. That mountain of a man probably doesn't even need Joe's help."

Having personally witnessed Davis carry a couch up to the second floor with no assistance, I had to nod in agreement.

The three of us were in the kitchen drinking coffee, getting acquainted, and enjoying several of Frannie's macarons, when Davis arrived.

He'd become my regular handyman, and the ox-shouldered teddy bear of a man now felt comfortable letting himself in. I poured him a coffee and apologized that the treat pickings were so slim.

His green eyes danced, and he brushed away my concerns with a wave of his enormous hand. "Don't worry about it, Sydney. I didn't come to eat all your food. I came to help out." He smiled warmly as he gulped down his coffee.

Joe hopped up from the table and took his mug to the sink. "You ready to get started, Davis?"

Davis did a couple of comical deep knee bends and cracked his knuckles. "Promise me you're not going to trip over your own feet, all right, buddy?"

Joe blushed adorably and nodded. "I'll be on my best behavior, Squatchy."

Covering my mouth with one hand, I failed to stifle my laughter. "Squatchy? Is there a story behind that nickname? Because if there is, I must hear it."

Cheryl winked and nodded at Joe. "Tell her, honey."

Joe dramatically cleared his throat and took a deep breath. "I was a senior when Davis was a freshman. I'd been taking a beating behind my inadequate center during our early summer practices, and even told the coach that I wanted to switch to kicker." He paused for effect and I gave him a blank look. "You had brothers, didn't you? I'm talking about football. I was the quarterback."

"Oh, oh, yeah, got it. I'm totally up to speed now. Continue." I had to cover another smile as he launched back into his dramatic re-telling.

"The next day, this beast walked onto the field." He gestured toward Davis and shaded his eyes as though trying to see the top of a tall tree. "I took one look and shouted, 'I'll stay on as quarterback if you put that Sasquatch in as center.' The team went nuts, and the name stuck."

Davis shook his head. "I didn't like it at first, but when the cute senior girls started wearing 'Squatchy' T-shirts and chanting for me at the games, I got on board."

Shaking my head, I grinned up at him. "And a legend was born. How come you never married any of those cute girls?"

For the first time since I met him, Davis seemed to close up. "We better get started. What are we looking for, Sydney?"

I knew better than to push. Everyone had a right to their secrets. "The event will be staged in the ballroom, and I've placed purple sticky notes on everything that needs to go down there. You can leave the smaller stuff for me and Cheryl, but all the big stuff is you guys. Got it?"

They both nodded, and Davis threw an arm around Joe. The normal-sized man looked like a small child next to the massive son of the local hardware store owner.

While the boys got busy moving things from the upper floors, Cheryl pointed toward the driveway and the sound of gravel crunching under tires. "Were you expecting anyone else?"

"Hm, I invited Augusta Adams over to authenticate a couple of things, and Frannie said something about tables—"

The doorbell chimed in its deep, sonorous bass, and Cheryl hustled to the front door. "Come in. Come in," she called from the entrance. "Sydney, do you want these tables from the church in the ballroom?"

I walked across the polished parquet floor and mentally ran through the setup I had planned. "Let's leave one table upfront for check-in. We want people to sign in during the preview so we can keep track of who returns. Then the rest of the tables can go to the ballroom. Nice straight lines. Nice wide aisles."

Cheryl offered me a haphazard salute and led the way around the imperial staircase to the massive, domed-ceiling ballroom at the back of the manor.

While Cheryl oversaw the table placement, I welcomed Augusta Adams, founder and master instructor at the Adams School of Colonial Arts. "Good morning, Augusta." Her full-figure and stern brown eyes commanded attention. "There were a couple of pieces that I honestly couldn't place. If the items are valuable enough to go to the live auction, I want to make sure I have an excellent description written up for Mia."

She offered a curt nod, removed her earmuffs, and gifted me a rare smile. "Smart. Mia Jones could call ships in from sea with that voice."

Classic Augusta. She always spoke her mind, regardless of the outcome. But I needed her expertise, and I'd have to put up with honesty—however blunt it might be.

I led the way to the delicate desk in the second-floor lavender room. The space also contained a dressing table, a highboy set of drawers, and an enormous wardrobe. The desk made the room feel crowded, and it seemed like overkill.

As soon as we entered Augusta began shaking her head. "That is absolutely not nineteenth century."

"How so?"

She proceeded to point out construction techniques, stain color, and lacquer consistency to support her assertion. I made careful notes of everything she described and thanked her before we headed off to examine a piece in another room.

Pointing to what I hoped would be my golden ticket, I offered my hypothesis. "I think this next item is called a dentist's cabinet. I have no idea what it's doing in the manor, and I can't imagine what sort of dentistry they would've been doing, but if it's genuine, it will fetch a great price at the auction."

Augusta followed me—remaining silent. She was clearly unwilling to engage in hypothetical conversations. Her expert judgment would be reserved until she saw it with her own two eyes.

When we entered the sitting room, she picked out the item immediately. "Now this is a gorgeous piece. Circa 1836. Quarter-sawn oak. Brass knobs. And it has been well cared for—not a scratch in sight. Your assumption was dead on. That's an authentic dentist's cabinet." She fanned out the tray-like drawers, carefully checked all the hardware, and nodded thoughtfully. "They probably moved it into the sitting room as a place for the ladies to keep their needlepoint. Perhaps each woman had her own drawer, and in that way, they could continue working on their specific projects without confusion."

It was a lovely piece of furniture, and Augusta's

fanciful guess at its ultimate purpose surprised me. I wouldn't have expected it from her. I glanced around the over-crowded space.

Yet, once again, there were too many lovely pieces of furniture in this room, and I wanted more space. Frannie and I had drawn several furniture layout options on paper before I made the final decisions on which pieces to sell. The ghosts had no sentimental favorites in this room, other than certain portraits, so I'd hoped the dentist's cabinet was the real deal. Augusta's endorsement gave me a boost of hope.

If the whole estate sale went well, and I gained a bit of a reputation as an antiques expert in the area, this might prove more than a onetime money grab. I might be able to promote myself as a personal antiques shopper and make a consistent living hunting down rare finds and vetting them for wealthy collectors. That sort of gig appealed to me for multiple reasons.

Augusta asked if she could peruse the items already in the ballroom, and I had to say yes. Even though the official preview started tomorrow, I could hardly withhold a reward for the free services she'd delivered.

"While you're doing that, I'm going to check on

Davis and Joe. Feel free to look at all of the items. Let me know if you see anything you like."

Augusta hurried away without a glance back.

The preparations were humming along. So I snuck up to the blue room to take another quick peek at the dagger. When I entered my room, I could've sworn there was a welcoming hum coming from the wrapped blade on the side table.

After uncovering it, I drew it from its sheath and admired the fine etching.

You look amazing in that sweater.

"Thank you." I grinned and slipped the blade back into the scabbard. Before I finished wrapping the silk, an additional comment pulsed from the delicate blade.

But you would look so much more fetching in a fitted button-down blouse.

That was new. Yesterday was all compliments and no suggestions. Although, after a moment of thought, I had to agree with the fashion tip. Even in the chilly manor, all the physical exertion of prep day was making me a little warm in my thick sweater. Maybe I could make a quick switch into one of my blouses—to be more comfortable.

10

The team had done a fantastic job yesterday. They organized everything in the ballroom to perfection. There was a section for standard shopping, a section for the silent auction, and the items for the live auction sat behind a curtained area. The whole thing would be interactive to keep the shoppers' interest straight through to the main event.

The preview would officially open in thirty minutes. I was nervous and excited. In exchange for allowing the ghosts to keep the items of their choosing, they promised to behave themselves today. No cold spots, no frost on mirrors, and no flickering lights. Nothing to scare potential buyers away.

Dagger had mentioned wearing a dress, but I knew I'd be on my feet for hours, and the thought of doing that all in dress-worthy four-inch heels didn't entice me. However, I'd selected a lovely blouse, fitted slacks, and gorgeous leather boots with *three*-inch heels. Plus, I left the natural curl in my hair, scooped it into a thick side-braid that draped over my shoulder and clasped it with one of Beatrix de Haviland's lovely brooches.

Finally, the doorbell chimed and interrupted my incessant pacing. I swept both double doors wide and opened my mouth to offer a warm greeting, but when my eyes took in the tableau on my terrace, my tongue refused to move.

"So it's true." Lucas Aconite in all of his six-foot, two-inch glory stood before me. His subtly highlighted brown hair was freshly coiffed and his flirty hazel eyes scanned up and down my body. "When Poppy showed me the article, I thought she was joking. But here you are, running estate sales in Maine. How quaint."

With as tightly as I gripped the handles of the front door, my knuckles had to be white. I wanted to reach across the threshold and slap the smug grin from his face, but at the mention of Poppy, my uncooperative voice continued to evade me while my eyes scanned over his girl du jour standing next to him. I gritted my teeth.

She didn't smile. Smiling was obviously beneath her. She was thin as a rail, nothing more than a hanger for her designer clothes—and her head was shaved. Admittedly, I kind of admired the bravery inherent in the bold hair choice, but I wouldn't let her know. Her eye makeup was perfection, but the extra-long false eyelashes were a bit much for Misty Meadows.

Lucas chuckled and pretended to shiver. "Aren't you going to invite us in from the cold, Sydney?"

I blinked once, wrenched my hands from the handles, and stepped back from the doors. "Welcome to Moonlight Manor. I'm the owner of the estate, and the current items on preview are in the ballroom. Let me show you the way." I chose not to acknowledge any of his other comments, but it was important to let him know that I *owned* this property. I wasn't just running around Maine willy-nilly, setting up estate sales for anyone. Also, just yesterday, I'd kind of been hoping that this venture might turn into a career of sorts, but that was none of his business.

As we walked through the grand mansion, Lucas was impressed. I could tell, because he kept his mouth shut, even with Poppy trailing after him. Whenever he thought something was beneath him, he would always run his mouth. Constantly talking about art installations he'd seen in Barcelona and let me assure you that was pronounced with the "T-H." *Barthelona.*

"This place is amazing. How can you afford it?"

Wow. I had never heard Lucas Aconite say anything so tacky. I had him on the ropes, and I liked him there. "The section at that end of the ballroom will be available for immediate sale tomorrow. These four rows of tables contain the items that will be on silent auction. And if you'd like to see the items that will be available for the live auction, they are behind the drapes."

I kept my head up and gestured like a bored flight attendant. "I'll be in the drawing room if you have any questions." Turning on my three-inch boot heels, wishing they were five-inch Manolos, I forced myself to saunter to the drawing room.

Once inside, I popped the secret passage open, ran upstairs to the burgundy room, and hissed for Sir Bogart.

He appeared a moment later. "You appear distressed, mistress."

I flapped my arms to maybe help leach the adrenaline-fueled panic from me. "Bogey. What am I going to do? He's here. He's here in my house—and he brought *her*."

Sir Bogart sniffed, and his ears flicked twice. "Mistress, I regret to inform you that names will be required if I am to follow this journey through your asylum."

"Right. Sorry. That man just—" My hands balled into fists, and I gave a silent scream that would make Edvard Munch blush. "Okay. Much better than the flapping. Lucas Aconite—the supreme jerk that cheated on me, dumped me, and fired me—is downstairs."

Bogey's golden eyes sparkled with mischief. "Would you like us to teach him a lesson, mistress?"

"Part of me does. But I don't think so. I'd rather impress him. Does that sound lame? Does that make me weak?"

He leapt onto the burgundy and gold duvet and sighed. "The only person you need to impress is yourself. This man sounds like a scoundrel unworthy of your attention. Is he here alone?"

I ground my teeth together. "Of course not. Lucas is never alone. He brought some twig of a woman with him, and she's wearing the very latest haute couture. Did I mention she has a shaved head?" I reached my hands toward the heavens in a silent plea for mercy. "She looks amazing. She doesn't have to spend all her life flat-ironing her hair. But he's so superficial. What could he possibly see in someone like Poppy?"

Sir Bogart yawned loudly. "Mistress, I suggest you stick to our original plan. Run the estate sale on your terms, and continue to build a new life for yourself. Is that not what you desire?"

His subtle reference to the Dagger of Desire did not go unnoticed. "You're right, Bogey. Thanks for the advice." Without delay, I hustled to the blue room and drew the dagger.

Your beauty is matched only by your intelligence. However, a dress would be more becoming.

I slipped the dagger back into its sheath and quivered. "I know. If I'd been wearing one of my really expensive frocks, she wouldn't be able to hold a candle to me. But I also couldn't change now. That would be super obvious. Tomorrow, I'm definitely wearing designer labels."

It was difficult to resist the urge to flat-iron my hair, but any edits I made to my appearance now would only prove to Lucas that he had thrown me off balance. I wasn't about to give him that satisfaction.

Instead, I proudly walked to the top of the imperial staircase and descended as though I were a bride walking down the steps of the New York Public Library, taking my time and demanding to be noticed.

Lucas and his eighty pounds of arm candy came click-clacking across the floor. He looked up and grinned lasciviously. "Poppy, wait in the Mercedes."

Her facial expression never changed, but the hurried click-clack of her six-inch platform heels told its own story.

He approached the bottom step, placed his hand on the thick banister, and gazed up at me with unmasked intentions. "A little time in the country has made you irresistible."

If I could puke directly on his Ferragamos, I would have. However, I wasn't willing to risk my fine hardwood floor. "I hope you enjoyed the preview, Mr. Aconite. The sale begins tomorrow at 10:00 a.m. Will you and your date be returning?"

Lucas grinned wickedly. "I'd be happy to come back all by my lonesome, if you promise to keep me company."

The man had the tongue of a serpent, and I wasn't completely immune to his flattery. But I refused to engage. "Will there be anything else? I have other preview guests to prepare for."

He wiggled his eyebrows and made a disgusting guttural sound, which I'm sure he thought would entice me. "See you tomorrow, Syd."

I arched an eyebrow. "I'm looking forward to your participation in the auction, Mr. Aconite."

11

Throughout the day, a steady stream of locals poured in, under the guise of previewing, but it was clear from their tendency to wander away from the main event in the ballroom, that most were primarily interested in catching a glimpse of Moonlight Manor's legendary ghosts. Though, as agreed, none of my spectral housemates made an appearance.

It was almost time to wrap things up for the day, and I felt great about it. This event looked as though it would be more than worth my time. I wasn't sure we'd sell out entirely, but it would come close enough.

After all the foot traffic and the greedy gazes of

the looky-loos, I thought it would be best to secure the manor fully for the evening. As I approached the beautiful double doors at the front entrance, I paused to admire the gorgeous stained-glass panels on either side. The earth-tone color palette, and the detail of the beautiful oak leaves, added a warm and welcoming border to the grand entrance.

The doorbell chimed, and my hand flinched above the handle. Hoping to turn away these last stragglers, I only opened one of the doors, and didn't offer my "Welcome to Moonlight Manor" catchphrase. "Sorry folks, the preview has ended for today. But the sale and auction re-open at 10:00 a.m. tomorrow."

The textbook blonde bimbo clutched her sugar daddy and made googly eyes while she whined in a baby voice. "Please, Kenny. Please. For me."

That's when the sickening hit of recognition slugged me in the gut. My new neighbor, Kenny Holt, was standing on my porch with a much younger, much hotter female companion. The powerful Manhattan mogul had dragged his midlife crisis well into his sixties. He had the obligatory hair plugs, the too-black dye job, an obvious eye tuck, and various facial fillers.

He reached toward his left wrist and adjusted his diamond-encrusted Rolex. "The ad said the preview was open until four. My watch is never wrong." He then proceeded to extend his right hand and introduced himself. "Kenny Holt. Your new neighbor."

For now, it seemed prudent to play dumb. What were the odds he would know who I am? I didn't even look like New York Sydney anymore. "Oh, good afternoon, Mr. Holt. I didn't realize that rundown property next door was for sale."

He sniffed sharply and puffed up his chest. "Wait till you see what Kenny Holt can do to that place. When I'm finished, it'll sparkle like the Hope diamond."

It was far more likely that it would stink like the Playboy mansion, but I kept that comment to myself. "I was planning on closing a little early, but since we're neighbors, come on in." I stepped back, and as Ms. Double-D cups entered, I smiled and introduced myself. "Hey. I didn't catch your name."

She swept a thick swath of her platinum-blonde extensions over her shoulder and smiled like a brainless fashion doll. "No, you couldn't. I hadn't told you yet, silly." She fluttered her eyelashes at me. "I'm Candi, with an 'i.' " She didn't offer her hand. Instead, she just giggled.

Of course it's with an "i." And I can imagine her dotting each of them with a little hand-drawn heart. I pushed the judgment aside. None of that really mattered at the end of the day. They were here for the auction, and I knew very well that Kenny Holt had some seriously deep pockets.

I gestured toward the rear of the manor. "Follow me to the ballroom, and I'll show you what items will be up for auction tomorrow."

When we entered the ballroom, even the vainglorious Kenny Holt had to catch his breath. He quickly covered his genuine amazement with a command to his concubine. "Go take a look at the jewelry, sweetie. Kenny will buy you something real nice."

I had just enough time to roll my eyes before he returned his attention to me.

"Show me the good stuff, Sydney. Kenny Holt doesn't mess around with antique irons and washbasins."

Wow. "Right this way, Mr. Holt." I took him behind the curtained area and headed directly to the dentist's cabinet. "This is one of the rarest items that will be on auction tomorrow. It's in immaculate condition and has been authenticated by a local expert."

"I'll take it," he snapped, nearly before I'd finished speaking.

"Oh, I hope you will. The bids for this will be lively at the auction tomorrow. Again, the live auction starts at noon, but the big-ticket items will be held for the end. There will also be plenty of silent auction items, and others available for immediate purchase."

He crossed his arms over his puffed-up chest, and whether his face was red from anger or high blood pressure, I couldn't be sure. "I'll take immediate purchase of this item."

"I'm terribly sorry, Mr. Holt. That's not how auctions work." Wow, if anything, this man had gotten more annoying with time.

"Hey, rules don't apply to Kenny Holt. What do you want for it? Fifty thousand?"

Every bone in my body wanted to take the money and run, but there were far too many previewers who'd commented about the dentist's cabinet. If I sold it before the live auction, it would definitely hurt my reputation.

I crossed my arms. "Mr. Holt, if you are willing to throw down bids like that, I'm absolutely sure you'll be able to beat out Lucas Aconite." I hated to say that man's name, but I knew it would push all the right buttons. And I was not disappointed. "But you'll understand if I am obligated to give everyone a chance at the item."

"What? Aconite is here?" The man glanced over his shoulder as though he expected Lucas to jump out from around a corner.

"He is. Mr. Aconite was the first one on-site today. He spent quite a long time previewing items, and he showed particular interest in this cabinet." That was a bald-faced lie. I needed Mr. Holt to leave, but I also needed him to come back tomorrow.

He took a sharp breath. "That snake. I'll be back tomorrow. Kenny Holt doesn't back down. I'll be back, and I'll win this bid."

"That's the spirit, Mr. Holt. I look forward to seeing you tomorrow."

He was shorter in person than I remembered. And when he turned to make his grand exit, the lovely lighting in the ballroom glinted off of his bald spot. I chuckled silently.

He snapped his fingers. "Candi. Candi, get your tight little tushy over here right now. We're leaving."

Candi seemed to have the attention span of a Labrador puppy, and it did not thrill me to discover that she'd been wandering freely through my home.

Before I could work myself into a tizzy, the

bleached-blonde extensions and micro miniskirt appeared at the top of the imperial staircase. "Kenny. I want this."

In her hand, she held the Dagger of Desire. She came snooping through my home and took a dagger from my private room. My dagger.

"That item is not for sale, Candi. The only items for sale are in the ballroom." Clenching my fists, I closed the distance to the grand entrance and marched up the stairs.

As I climbed, she tried her silly, flirty tricks on me, but it was going to take more than cleavage and some batting eyelashes to convince me to give up my dagger.

She danced in place and waved the dagger under my nose. "Oh, Sydney. I just love it. Kenny will pay you whatever you want. He loves to buy things for me."

When I reached her side, I snatched the dagger from Candi's perfectly manicured hands and pointed to the front door with the sheathed tip. "The preview is now closed. You and Mr. Holt are welcome to return tomorrow when the auction begins. 10:00a.m. Once again, this item is not for sale, and you will be required to stay within the approved locations during the sale. If you do not, you will be asked to leave and escorted from the property."

Candi sulked down the stairs in a snit, and Kenny mumbled all sorts of financial promises as they exited the manor. I closed my fist around the dagger and glared as tail lights disappeared down the drive.

12

Rising two hours earlier than normal, I had one cup of coffee for breakfast, and flat-ironed my hair into a glistening waterfall. It had been such a long time since I'd last heat-treated my hair, meaning my tresses really soaked it up. Feeling quite pleased, I beamed at myself in the mirror.

The space-dyed, ribbed-knit midi dress I'd selected was meant to emphasize all of my best features. However, my multiple diet cheats since I arrived in Misty Meadows added a cushion around my middle that resulted in the need to double-up on my Spanx to get the desired shape. I completed the outfit with gorgeous five-inch Manolos.

When I picked up the dagger, it was truly pleased with my choices.

You look stunning. Poppy isn't worthy to stand in your shadow.

"Exactly. Thank you, Dagger." I set the lovely blade on the bed and selected a pair of gold teardrop earrings to accent my look. A familiar voice interrupted my final check in the mirror. Although, that one last look was hardly necessary. I knew how great I looked, and pleasure hummed through me, and I deserved great things.

"Sydney, come on down. I got cupcakes."

When I reached the top of the stairs, Frannie nearly dropped her pink pastry box. "Syd, is that you? Holy moly, girl. What exactly are you selling today?" She giggled and winked as she opened the lid of the pastry box to show me the contents. "I brought your favorite."

I descended with casual elegance. "Oh, no thank you. I couldn't possibly. I've already had breakfast. Thank you, though. You're too kind."

Frannie's expression was a mix of confusion and hurt. "What's going on? Why are you acting stiff like that? Did the preview go badly? It's not like you to turn down my famous caramel-apple cupcakes."

When I reached the bottom step, I swept my

shimmering locks behind my shoulder. "The preview was fantastic. In fact, there's sure to be a bidding war over the dentist's cabinet. It'll be my top earner this time. My new neighbor is desperate to get his hands on it, and once I mention that to Lucas—"

She froze in the middle of the grand foyer and nearly crunched her bright pink box. "Lucas," she hissed. "Your ex-boyfriend was here yesterday, and you didn't call me?" She scooped an arm around my shoulders and attempted to escort me to the kitchen. "Do you want to talk about it?"

I shrugged off her arm and dismissed the mention of Lucas with a flick of my wrist. "It was nothing. I'm totes over him. I'm just eager to see if I can start a bidding war."

Frannie narrowed her gaze. "What is up with you? You're acting really strange."

I laughed and tossed my hair again. "It's just me, living my best life. Obvs."

She swallowed, looked at the ground, and walked to the kitchen. There was a tiny voice inside me whispering that I should go after her and apologize, but sleek-haired Sydney Coleman had no time for such nonsense. Feelings had no place in the equation right now. Not when there was money to be made.

My pricey heels click-clacked as I walked into the

ballroom to make sure everything was perfect. The setup remained just as I'd left it. Neither late visitor had changed or moved anything. I drew on my past skills as a social media marketer and all that had taught me about managing people's buying habits, throwing everything I knew into making the event layout absolutely perfect.

When Mia showed up to look over the script for the live auction, she walked right past me. I had to call her name three times before she would believe that it was me. Even then, she seemed dubious about my identity. Proof positive that I'd outdone myself. This was going to be a day for the record books.

The doors opened promptly at 10:00, and a sizable crowd had already gathered outside Moonlight Manor near the front yard fountain. I guided them to the ballroom and returned to the check-in table to offer Frannie some last-minute instruction.

I pointed to her. "Be sure to check their name off the list if they came for the preview day. And remember to offer everyone a paddle for the live auction, even if they don't think they'd be interested. It will create more buzz if there are more people carrying paddles. Oh, and the live auction starts at noon."

Frannie nodded, but she didn't make eye contact. "Sure."

A self-satisfied sigh escaped as I passed toward the doors. It was true, good help was hard to find, and I deserved good help. Didn't I? Especially after all I'd been through since arriving in Misty Meadows.

At last, Lucas and Poppy arrived. I didn't plan on greeting them. I would wait until they stopped at the sign-in table, and then come up with a silly reason to stop and give Frannie some other instruction.

My plan might have worked, but Lucas caught sight of me through the crowd. "Poppy, check us in. I need to speak to Sydney."

He walked across the floor with the confidence of a jungle cat closing in on his prey. "Like I always said, you clean up real nice." He wiggled his eyebrows and grinned so big his hazel eyes sparkled handsomely.

For some reason, the gesture didn't sicken me today.

So I leaned close to him and lowered my voice. "I'm glad you were able to return for the auction, Mr. Aconite. I shouldn't tell you this, but Kenny Holt's just purchased the property next door, and he showed up at the end of the day yesterday, eager to buy several items."

Lucas's chin snapped up, and he clenched his jaw. "Holt? In Maine? That—"

I raised my hand in fake apology. "Oh, I assumed you knew. He was particularly interested in the oak dentist's cabinet. He demanded I sell them to him before the auction, but I told him I had to give you a chance at them. Fair is fair after all." With that, I turned and walked like a runway model into the ballroom.

13

Sales were going well on the immediate-purchase items. Cheryl and Joe both appeared quite busy running the register and ringing out purchases. I walked around the silent auction tables, pleased to see the number of bids and the corresponding dollar amounts. This day was shaping up nicely.

Raised voices on the other side of the ballroom caught my attention. Oh dear, Kenny Holt had arrived, and he and Lucas were not pleased to see each other.

I strode across the ballroom and stepped between them. Towering over Kenny, but eye-to-eye with Lucas. "Now, now, boys. There will be plenty of time for you to show us who's in charge when the live auction starts. In the meantime, if you can't behave, I'll have you removed."

Lucas opened his mouth, but before he could utter some pathetic, testosterone-soaked phrase, I tipped my head toward Davis Martin. I hadn't officially asked him to serve as security, but since he was a natural introvert, he was already standing in a corner with his arms crossed. Squatchy looked the part, whether he was the part or not.

Lucas swallowed his terse comeback and scooped Poppy away before anyone could utter another word. Kenny glared at anyone and everyone who glanced his way. Though, his lady friend edged closer.

Candi pawed at my shoulder and cooed in my ear. "Oh, Sydney. I wish you would reconsider selling me that pretty, pretty knife. I just love sapphires. They're my favorite."

I wrenched myself out of her reach. "Sorry. There are several other gorgeous items. Please take another look around. I'm sure you'll find something that you can fall in love with."

She moaned like a spoiled child, but I didn't have time for her ridiculous nonsense.

Returning to the grand entrance, I gazed over the sign-in sheet and estimated nearly one hundred and fifty people were on site. The serious collectors had come in early on preview day and would arrive in time for the live auction. Most of them had no interest in anything but the auction items. So we might have accumulated close to two-hundred interested parties at the estate when all was said and done. Perhaps I would be able to keep the lights on longer than I originally believed possible. A rousing success would make such a venture repeatable. It would also make my life here at Moonlight Manor sustainable. Plus I *deserved* it.

I turned to leave the table, but Frannie gripped my hand. "Syd, is everything okay? I saw your ex-boyfriend, and the girl he brought with him. It must bother you a little. I can get someone to watch the sign-in desk if you need to talk."

I patted her on the shoulder and shrugged. "Oh, thank you soooo much. I'm more than fine. I promise. Super okay. Totes."

She nodded, but the look in her eyes wreaked of disbelief as she slipped away. "Totes," she murmured. "Totes."

The shopping area was getting cleaned out fast, and tables were starting to look barer. It looked like folks didn't much care what they got their hands on, as long as they got a piece of the area's haunted mansion to call their own. Fine by me.

The live auction was about to begin, and the din in the ballroom increased in intensity. Each attendee seemed excited, and everybody had a bidding paddle. I watched with pleasure as Kenny Holt took a seat in the front row's prime real estate. However, his arm *candy* was missing.

When I glanced over my shoulder, I saw her practically running to the front door. In those stiletto heels, with her imbalanced body, a top-heavy girl like that could really injure herself. Huh. What was the big rush?

As soon as she saw me, she smiled as though I were the sun and the moon. "Sydney. You're the best. The absolute best. I'm racing back to put this in the safe, and then I'll see you for drinks. Kenny said he owes you big time."

I glanced at the plain paper sack in her hand, but had no idea what she was talking about.

I would discover the truth all too soon.

14

Mia's loud voice echoed from the ballroom. "Take your seats," she boomed. "We begin in five, four, three, two..."

The time had finally come. No one wanted to miss a minute of the excitement, including me. Any last empty seats quickly filled in.

Mia slammed the gavel she'd borrowed from a judge she knew, and they wheeled out the first item —a large mother-of-pearl inlaid jewelry box. The crowd hushed as she read the description, made a joke, and began the bidding at the number I'd requested.

The energy of the crowd was palpable. As I moved around the room, it became obvious that I'd picked the right person for the job of auctioneer. Mia was hamming it up for the audience and egging the bidders on with friendly jokes and thinly veiled bribes.

By the end, the large mother-of-pearl inlaid jewelry box went for twice what I'd hoped. And so did the next two items. This day was even more spectacular than I'd dreamed it would be. I would be able to get some new tires for Blue Bell. Or . . . I blinked as a thought struck me. Maybe even something sleeker than that old nearly broken-down pick-up truck. Something more like Sydney deserved to drive.

The crowd laughed about some joke Mia told, and they brought out the next item. I needed to check on the others before settling in to observe whatever bidding war we could get going between the well-moneyed rivals. Since it was the most unique and high-dollar item, the dentist's cabinet would be the next-to-last item presented.

Slipping along the back of the crowd, I made my way toward Cheryl and Joe. She waved eagerly when she saw me approaching. I smiled. "How did you guys do?"

She grinned from ear to ear and patted Joe on the back. "Joe was fantastic. He kept pushing the haunted mansion angle, and telling folks what great

Christmas gifts everything would make. We sold out before Mia even started the live auction. I lost count, but I know we made over two thousand dollars."

Joe beamed. "I just made a pass down the rows of silent auction items, and there are some hefty sums on those bidding sheets. You really know what you're doing, Sydney."

It felt good to be complimented for something I'd done all on my own. And it didn't hurt to look absolutely fantastic while receiving the compliment. I thanked them and returned my attention to the live auction. Items were going fast, and the bids were nicely bloated, too. When Mia finally got to the dentist's cabinet, I held my breath.

She opened the bidding at five thousand, and Lucas Aconite immediately bid ten. Several people clapped. Kenny Holt topped that with a bid of fifteen thousand, and the crowd gasped. I stifled a grin. This is what I'd wanted. With these two expensive egos in the crowd, I'd hoped for the best, and they had not disappointed.

No one else was even in the mix. The two power-mad Manhattanites volleyed the bid back and forth, topping each other by five thousand per bid, as though it was nothing.

When the bid reached fifty thousand, Mia patted

her chest and shook her head. "You two guys have taken this to, what I like to call, a whole other level." She polled the audience at large to see if there were any late bloomers that wished to enter the battle, but there were no takers.

Lucas had tired of the game. He stood up and announced he would pay one hundred thousand for the cabinet. Beside him, Poppy rolled her eyes, but Lucas didn't see it.

I nearly fainted. That was . . . that was more than I hoped to get out of the whole auction. There were quite a few people holding their breath at this point, waiting to see if his adversary would counter.

Kenny Holt angrily threw his bidding paddle on the floor and stormed out of the ballroom. Candi scurried after him. She waved at me before she disappeared around the corner.

Lucas smirked at his retreating foe and waited for Mia to finalize his bid on that item.

"That's one hundred thousand going once, going twice, and sold to number 124." Her borrowed gavel hovered over the lectern I'd found tucked in one of the third-floor bedrooms.

Lucas searched the room for me, but I ducked into a crowd of people and avoided his gaze. I had no interest in him pretending that his bid was some kind of charitable donation. The only reason he bid that high was to utterly crush Kenny Holt. If Lucas had any authentic human emotions, he wouldn't have cheated on me in the first place or dumped me or thrown me out of our apartment in the city. No amount of money was going to erase that wound. However, there was a certain lovely karma about taking his money and using it to pay for my long-term upkeep.

He left the hyped energy in the ballroom, returned with a paid ticket from Frannie, and waved it around for all to see. A smattering of applause filtered through the attending crowd. Then he walked directly up to Davis Martin and handed him a wad of cash. For a moment I was confused, but when I saw Davis round up a buddy and watched as the two of them carted the dentist's cabinet out of the ballroom, it became clear. Lucas had hired some underlings to do his bidding. Classic.

Poppy strutted out in his wake, and I hoped they would head directly back to the city. I had no interest in being subjected to any more of his sleazy advances, or her creepy, emotionless stares.

The live auction wrapped up with the final item, and Mia announced that the silent auction bidding would close in thirty minutes. I hadn't asked her to speed up the time frame, but it made sense. The live auction had moved much quicker than any of us had expected, so closing the silent auction early would allow us to clean up at a reasonable hour.

Once the day was done and all purchases had been paid for and removed, it shocked me to see the only thing remaining in the ballroom was the grand piano.

I asked my helpers to hang around and offered to open a bottle of champagne, but there were no takers. Even Frannie shook her head. "Thanks, Sydney. I have to open early tomorrow. I'll see you when I see you."

She didn't exactly look at me when she said her goodbyes. Maybe one of the customers was rude to her, or maybe Lucas said something inappropriate to her. Well, not my problem. She was a grown woman, wasn't she? She could take care of herself.

The two men from the church would return in the morning to pick up the tables, so after Joe and Cheryl left, I locked the front door and headed up to my room to change into something more comfortable.

When I stepped into the blue room, my eyes darted to the bed, to the place where I'd left my little cheerleader on the duvet. The silk wrap was folded into a neat square, and the Dagger of Desire was nowhere to be seen.

My heart skipped a beat as panic flooded me. No whispered encouragements would bolster my mood. My upper lip curled into a ferocious snarl. How could the bed be bare? Who could have taken *my* dagger?

Turning, I raced out of the room and shouted for my ghostly roommates. It had been a couple of months since I'd run in heels, and I was out of practice. Luckily, the thick banister provided a ready handhold, which prevented me from falling down the stairs and seriously injuring myself.

Sir Bogart was the first to answer my call, and he appeared on the bottom of the handrail, on the newel post. His tail flicked around the baluster. "The empty ballroom seems a positive indication of your success, mistress."

I studied the suspicious feline. "Did you take the dagger? I know how much you didn't want me to have it. Did you send anyone else to take it?"

He lifted his chin and shook his head. "I saw nothing. And I find your tone offensive."

"Sorry. I don't have time for niceties. Someone stole the dagger from my room."

Velma appeared nearby with a hand cupped over

her mouth. Her glowing eyes darkened with guilt. "Beggin' your pardon, miss."

"For what?" I stepped toward her as an inexplicable rage boiled within me. "What did you do?"

She cowered, and her apparition flickered. "I was straightening up, miss. And I saw the pretty knife, and I thought you must've forgotten to put it in the ballroom. So I slipped in there and put it on the table before anyone could see."

"The table? You sold the Dagger of Desire for a pittance?" My hands balled into fists. "It was priceless. That was *my* dagger. Mine. Do you understand?"

She trembled without answering.

Inside, I seethed. How could one punish a ghost servant for taking liberties she shouldn't have?

Norman appeared, placed a soothing arm around Velma's shoulders, and escorted her to the kitchen. "She knew nothing of the dagger's true value, madam," he offered over his shoulder. "It was an honest mistake."

Fuming, I marched after them. "You could have asked. You should have asked. Nothing in this house belongs to you. Any of you."

Norman didn't answer, and Velma whimpered quietly.

Sir Bogart intercepted me before I could reach the

kitchen and sent an icy chill over my whole body. "Miss Coleman, I warned you about the dagger's power. Look at yourself. Look at what you've become."

Glancing toward a large mirror on the opposite wall, I hardly recognized my reflection. My face was contorted with anger and jealousy. My sleek black hair and snug fitting dress were echoes of the past, a former version of myself I liked no longer. This wasn't who I was anymore.

I stopped short and smoothed my hand over my hair. A cringe contorted my face. I'd referred to Velma as a servant rather than my friend, and I'd reverted to what I'd despised about being in New York. What on earth was going on?

Before Bogey could offer any additional comments, snippets of my interactions with Frannie blasted to the front of my consciousness, and I gasped as my eyes widened.

"Yes?" Sir Bogart hissed.

"I was perfectly horrible to Frannie." I leaned over, unbuckled my shoes, and ran upstairs in my bare feet to retrieve my phone. She had to forgive me.

I tried her several times, but there was no answer. Opting for a text, I offered a heartfelt apology and begged her to answer my call. When I called again, she didn't answer, and I stared at the blank screen. Had I hurt her feelings that much?

Instead of the silent treatment I feared, she called me. Before I could get a word out, she asked, "What's going on with you, Sydney?"

Through apologetic tears, I explained the dagger's influence. How I'd fallen under its insidious spell, and let it bring out the very worst in me. I must've apologized at least seven times.

She stopped me before I could eke out an eighth apology. "I knew something was off. You really hurt my feelings, Syd. I felt like that freckle-face, carrot-top kid in elementary school all over again. That dagger did a number on you."

"I know. And the worst part is, Velma accidentally put it in the ballroom this morning. Someone—"

The memory of Candi oozing gratitude as she raced out of the manor came flashing back. *Oh, no. No, no, no. Candi. It had to be her.* Dread curled in my stomach.

"What is it? Sydney, are you still there?"

I groaned loudly. "I think I know who bought the dagger."

"Who?"

"My new next-door neighbor's bimbo girlfriend. Or I suppose I should say, Kenny Holt bought it for her. She took it from my room on preview day, and I told her it was not for sale. She must've lost her mind when she spotted it on the tables today."

Frannie mumbled something about how I was better off without it.

"I hear what you're saying, Frannie, and you're right. Again, I'm very sorry for my behavior. But it's not safe for anyone to have. We should put it right back in that secret compartment in the tower room."

"Maybe you can just head next-door and talk to your new neighbors. They might sell it back to you."

Sighing heavily, I shook my head as I replied. "After the humiliation that Kenny suffered in the live auction today? I don't think he's likely to do me any favors."

"You never know."

"Oh, I know, Fran."

Bless Frannie's heart, she tried to encourage me anyway. "It can't hurt to ask, Syd."

15

No time like the present. I changed out of my uncomfortable undergarments and opted for a pair of stretch denim and a lovely cable-knit sweater. I raided the kitchen and discovered a couple of Frannie's cupcakes still in the pastry box. Since I was going next door to ask for a big favor, the least I could do was bring a peace offering. I bundled up and headed down the path from my backyard to the old Williams estate.

A luxurious Mercedes motorhome was parked on-site, with a generator humming away behind it. I approached the main door of the travel trailer and knocked firmly.

Candi, in nothing more than a loosely tied silk

robe, answered the door. "Hello, Sydney. Come in. Come in. I can't thank you enough."

Once inside the luxurious home on wheels, I offered her the box of cupcakes. She peeked inside and her eyes nearly popped out of her head. "Oh, I can't eat these. No dairy, no gluten, and no processed sugar." Candi pushed the box back toward me as though I'd offered her a porcupine. "How else can I keep my figure?"

"Sorry, I didn't know about your dietary restrictions." I didn't miss those days. The pressure of performance and keeping my figure as thin as I possibly could. "No" governed everything.

She smiled, and she seemed kinder than she had at Moonlight Manor. "It's fine. I'm used to having to tell people. Um, Kenny is in the sauna in the back. Is there something I can do for you?"

Here goes nothing. "The item that you purchased today was placed in the ballroom by mistake. I need to buy it back from you."

Her shoulders fell, and she whimpered like a small child. "But sapphires are my favorite."

"I know, Candi. And I'm so sorry. I'll pay you double. It just wasn't supposed to be sold today—or ever."

She wiped a finger under her kohl-rimmed eye

and moped toward a small table. She reached into the bag that I'd seen her carrying out of Moonlight Manor, retrieved the item, and brought it to me. She wasn't nearly as unlikable as she had seemed back at the manor, and I wondered if it had really been her or if it was the dagger.

"Are you sure, Sydney? Kenny will totally pay more if that's what you want."

I glanced at the item in her hand and it seemed the room was spinning. How had she not wound up with the cursed, whispering blade? "Where's the dagger?"

She tilted her head like a confused puppy. "What?"

"The dagger. Diamond and sapphire scabbard. That's the item I need back."

Candi shook her head and frowned. "I don't have it. You told me yesterday it wasn't for sale. And Kenny was offering you tons of money. I mean, he would've paid anything. But you said it wasn't for sale. So when I found this sapphire pendant, I thought it was a consideration prize."

"Do you mean consolation prize?"

Her collagen-injected lips made a pouty smile. "Yeah. That's the one. I thought you were, like, trying to make me feel better."

I did not have time for this woman and her entirely self-absorbed worldview. "Candi, do you swear to me that you don't have that dagger?"

"Absolutely, Sydney. After you did me this huge favor, I would never lie to you."

My head was spinning. "All right. I'm sorry to have bothered you. Do you want to keep the cupcakes for Kenny?"

She giggled and leaned toward me. "I don't let him eat that stuff," she whispered. "He's already got a little gut, you know?" She leaned back. "But don't tell him I said that."

I really didn't want to know anything about Kenny Holt's gut. "Well, thanks for coming to the auction today. Again, I'm so sorry I bothered you."

"No worries. Maybe we'll see each other around now that we're neighbors." She grinned like it was good news.

I smiled and nodded my way off the Williams estate. Then, clutching the pastry box under my arm like a football, I hurried home. Sheer panic fueled me, and I ran like a sled dog.

When I burst through the back door and into the mudroom, I announced my dilemma with shouts interspersed by gasps for air, and I called for my helpers. "It's not there. Can you believe it?"

The ghostly trio joined me within moments and gathered around me.

I panted as I still tried to catch my breath. "Bad news. Candi and Kenny did not buy the dagger. She bought a sapphire pendant. We have to figure out who bought that dagger."

Norman clasped his hands behind his back. "Perhaps the young couple manning the cashbox would remember, madam."

I rushed forward to hug him, but instead passed directly through his energy. Clearing my throat, I backed out of his . . . ether-ness. "Sorry, Norman. That was supposed to be a hug. That's brilliant. I'm gonna call Cheryl Johnson right now."

Cheryl couldn't remember the woman's name, but when she mentioned a shaved head, I knew exactly whom she meant. Three apparitions were waiting patiently beside me. "It was Poppy. That chick Lucas dragged up here, to try and make me jealous. Why did it have to be *her*? The last person in the world I want to have to call is Lucas Aconite."

I pinched the bridge of my nose. Norman frowned, and Velma asked if I wanted a spot of tea, but I waved them both away. Sir Bogart didn't speak at all, but at least he didn't utter a proper "I told you so" after he warned me about what a mess I might cause by taking the dagger out of the hidden apothecary. I had to solve it.

Pacing vigorously, I continued to mumble. "But I don't have any other way to get ahold of her. We have to get the dagger back. Maybe I could convince Frannie to give Lucas a call for us."

Sir Bogart sniffed, and I turned toward him. "What is it?"

"Have you apologized to Miss Clark?" He squeezed his eyelids and twitched his whiskers. "For giving in to the whims of the dagger?"

My cheeks flushed with embarrassment. "Yes. Multiple times. I was horrible. That dagger is absolutely as dangerous as you said, and I didn't even realize how much it had begun to change me and in so little time, too."

Sir Bogart inhaled sharply. "You have experienced but a fraction of the dagger's true pull. If it were to be wielded by a weaker-minded soul, its effects would be more potent. Thankfully, you are neither weak-minded nor inclined to violence. The incident to which Rosetta referred in her note was murder, mistress. The depths of the dagger's curse have not yet been reached. You must swallow your pride and call Mr. Aconite. Lives may depend on it."

A chill worked its way down my spine as I considered the glowing-eyed cat. He had a point, and I couldn't ignore his warning. Not now. Wordlessly, I retrieved my phone.

It embarrassed me to admit that over three months from the day Lucas Aconite fired and dumped me, I still had his number in my speed dial. I'd never bothered to remove it. Maybe I should have, but I had allowed it to linger in my phone. Three sets of eyes waited eagerly as the ringing echoed from the speaker on my cell phone.

"Voicemail. If that's not an admission of guilt, I don't know what is. He's obviously avoiding my calls for a reason. Lucas probably thinks that he deserved a bonus item because he overpaid for that piece of furniture." I gazed at the gathered faces and shrugged. "Based on his behavior at the auction, I really expected him to answer my call. Now what?"

Norman bowed slightly. "May I make a suggestion?"

"Of course. By all means."

He cleared his throat. "Perhaps you should consider contacting Sheriff Allen to report the theft. You could still continue your search, but it may be beneficial to have more people involved in the recovery."

"Yes, I suppose. I'm sure you're right. If I report

the dagger as missing or stolen, then I can also refer to the police report if it pops up somewhere else."

"Yes, miss," Norman agreed.

"It's just embarrassing to admit that he took advantage of me—again. Even if he didn't exactly know it." I stepped away from the ghosts and placed the call. When I explained the situation to Sheriff Allen, she was sympathetic, but requested that I come into the station to file a report. She couldn't justify coming to me this time since we didn't have a dead body or any otherwise urgent scenario.

"Hey, guys, I have to head into town to file the report."

They nodded and vanished. I returned to the portrait gallery to take a close-up picture of the dagger on Sir Edward's belt. The portrait was the only evidence I had of the item in question. Since it hadn't been officially part of the estate sale, I never took photos of it, so there was nothing posted online or printed in the flyers.

Grabbing the keys to Blue Bell, I headed outside and carefully followed Frannie's tracks out of the driveway. I let Blue Bell warm up a little since it was still cold out, but the snow wasn't as treacherous as it had been the morning after the sleepover. Nevertheless, I didn't want to wind up unintentionally off-roading.

About two miles from the house, the beams of my headlights bounced off a vehicle at an awkward angle in the ditch.

Wait.

I'd recognize that car anywhere—even in the dark. That was Lucas Aconite's Porsche. How long had it been stuck in the ditch? Pulling my foot off the accelerator, I eased to the shoulder and jumped out of my vehicle. He was probably out of practice with winter driving and had slid off the road.

As I approached the car, a growing unease swirled up from my stomach and tightened my chest. I tried his phone again, and could hear it ringing inside the car, but he made no move toward it. He didn't even turn his head to see who was calling.

When I reached the window, I shined the light from my phone into the darkened interior—and screamed.

Running back toward Blue Bell, I climbed inside and dialed 911. "Sheriff Allen, it's Sydney. I was on my way into town and noticed a vehicle on the side of the road. I thought I recognized it, so I pulled over to see if the occupants were all right."

Sheriff Allen asked for details about the make, model, and license plate number, but I couldn't be bothered with details. "Sheriff, you don't understand."

She paused.

"He's dead."

Now I had her attention.

"It's Lucas Aconite—" I lost control of my emotions. The sobbing and dry heaving took over. I don't remember if I mentioned where I was, but the line went dead and moments later, the distant echo of sirens filled the air.

The swirling blue and red lights of three patrol cars approached at high-speed. Two darted to the shoulder on the opposite side of the road. The deputies jumped out and lit flares. The third car pulled nose-to-nose with the Porsche.

Hopping down from the cab of my truck, I scrambled toward the Porsche.

I instantly recognized the tall, athletic form of Sheriff Haley Allen as she exited her cruiser and crossed in front of the headlights. "I need you to step away from the vehicle, Miss Coleman."

The shock of what she was saying somehow penetrated the fog of horror that had gripped me. "What are you saying? You don't think—"

"I need you to step away from the vehicle. Once

we've processed the crime scene, I'll be questioning you. I hope you have an alibi, Miss Coleman."

When she was close enough to hear me whisper, I leaned forward. "Sir Bogart is my alibi."

At the mention of the ghost cat she'd met as a child, her features softened. "I'll make a mental note of that. But you know that alibi won't hold up in court and cannot be entered into the official record." She motioned for me to step back, and I did so, reluctantly.

She directed her flashlight into the vehicle and completed a visual search.

"Is there a woman in the car? I was so scared when I saw Lucas slumped over the steering wheel—"

Sheriff Allen slipped off her winter gloves and replaced them with a pair of latex. She carefully opened the car door and peered inside. "Negative. No passenger. No one in the backseat." The sheriff turned toward me. "Was he traveling with a companion?"

The word companion got under my skin, but I couldn't afford to show any anger or agitation toward Lucas. "He came to the preview day of my estate sale and returned today to buy a large dentist's cabinet.

He was traveling with a woman named Poppy. Tall, thin, shaved head."

Sheriff Allen slowly straightened to her full height, turned toward me, and shook her head. "Are you telling me this man is your ex-boyfriend? The man who kicked you out of your apartment in New York?"

Bad news definitely travels fast in a small town. Who had told her *that*? "Yes. However, there was no animosity between us. Like I said, he came to the sale and paid outrageously for an item. Why would I kill him right after he decided to throw a small fortune at me? That wouldn't make any sense." Especially not right here by my home. Why would I do something like that here? I couldn't say any of that out loud, though, or it would make me seem more guilty.

She reached into the car, retrieved Lucas's cell phone, and looked at his recently missed calls. Once again, her eyes locked onto me with suspicion.

I pulled my coat around me more tightly. "What? Are you accusing me again? When I discovered the dagger was missing, I made several phone calls." There was no need for me to get into the details of why I suspected Lucas and his bald sidekick.

"This would be the dagger you called to report missing?" Sheriff Allen's lips pressed into a grim line.

"Yes. That's what I was trying to explain. I made a call to Lucas, along with several others I thought might have seen the dagger."

"Unfortunately, my initial examination indicates the victim was stabbed in the back."

"Stabbed? In the back? While driving?" Most of me could easily admit that Lucas had stabbed more than his share of people in the back, figuratively, but that didn't mean he deserved to be murdered. "Then you should probably talk to Kenny Holt. He's the guy who bought the Williams place. He and Lucas have a long-standing feud. They were bidding against each other on the cabinet. Lucas won the item, and Kenny Holt was furious when he left the auction. Ask Mia, she saw."

Sheriff Allen slipped the cell phone into an evidence bag and removed her latex gloves. "I doubt he has a piece of furniture stashed in this thing. Did you ship it back to New York for him?"

"No. He paid Davis Martin and some other guy to load it up for him. He must've called his own moving company. His agency uses a ton of vendors for events in the city. Davis should be able to confirm my story."

Sheriff Allen tilted her head and scoffed. "Sydney, no New York City vendor is gonna drive all the way to

Maine to pick up a piece of furniture. I don't care how important Mr. Aconite thought he was."

She had a point. "Fine, I'm sure if you check with the local company, he probably hired them. He would never ask me for help."

She adjusted her Smokey-Bear style hat and frowned. "I thought you said there was no animosity between the two of you? Why wouldn't he ask you for help?"

"I didn't mean it like that, Sheriff. Lucas didn't ask anyone for help. He was that kind of guy. He did everything on his own." I chewed my bottom lip as memories flashed in my head. Something about handcuffs clicking around my wrists the last time Sheriff Allen thought I'd committed murder. How many times did we have to go through this sort of thing?

Sheriff Allen considered me for a long while. She shifted from side to side, and her boots crunched on the snow. "You're free to go, Miss Coleman. But I have to follow the evidence on this case. If that trail leads back to you, there's not gonna be a second chance. I hope for your sake this Kenny Holt lead pans out." As she walked back to her cruiser, she turned and added one more instruction. "You may as well head into town and file that report on the missing dagger. In all likelihood, that dagger was the murder weapon. And, well, it's extremely uncanny that you're reporting it lost the very day it was used in the commission of homicide. If it's actually missing, you need to report it."

Nodding mutely, I returned to my car and drove five miles per hour under the speed limit, all the way into town. Sheriff Allen didn't have to tell me twice, but then again, I heard plenty in what she *wasn't* saying. A missing item report couldn't keep me out of jail, but maybe it would help if the dagger actually showed up with Lucas's blood on it.

I couldn't believe Lucas was dead. Poppy was missing, and I was a suspect in another murder. My stomach churned. All because of that stupid dagger.

After I filed the missing property report, I headed directly to the bakery.

16

When I found Frannie alone, wiping down the pastry case in her quaint little shop, relief hit me so hard I thought my knees might buckle. At least she would be a friendly face in the middle of my latest mess.

The scent of whatever late-night bake was in her oven wafted through the locked door. But the inviting aromas were lost on me. I was a bundle of nerves, and she immediately noticed me standing meekly outside the entrance. She tilted her head, shrugged, and rushed toward me as though she were a life preserver in a roiling sea.

She unlocked the door and motioned me inside. There was no friendly greeting. Once the door was secured, she spoke. "What's going on, Syd? I'd say you look like you saw a ghost, but since you live with them, I wouldn't think that sort of thing would scare you anymore."

"Lucas was murdered." My voice didn't crack when the three words slipped out, but my chin quivered.

Frannie's hand covered her mouth. She shook her head in disbelief and embraced me. "I'm so sorry, Sydney. I know things were over between the two of you, but at one point, he was pretty important to you."

Huge, wet tears tumbled down my cheeks. She handed me a napkin, and I tried to pull myself together. "It was awful. Sheriff Allen said he was stabbed in the back."

Her auburn eyebrow arched. "I hate to say it, but from everything I know about the man, he probably deserved it." She waved me to a table. "Do you want anything? Hot chocolate?"

Shaking my head, I took a deep breath and struggled to continue. "I told the sheriff that I thought Kenny Holt was to blame. I don't think Candi knew what he was up to, though. When I went over there to talk to her, she claimed they didn't have the dagger. I know I should probably question her, but she doesn't really seem smart enough for a complicated deception."

Frannie nearly choked on her reply. "I'm surprised that girl manages to find two shoes that match."

We chuckled, and I blew my nose. "We shouldn't make fun. She genuinely seems to care about Kenny. Or at least Kenny's money. She takes good care of him. I offered her some cupcakes, and she said she doesn't let him eat that kind of stuff."

My baker boss friend crossed her arms and pretended to fume. "Well, now I hate her even more."

An uncontrollable laugh erupted from my throat. "Thanks, I needed that. If it turns out the dagger is the murder weapon, that's gonna be real bad for me. My fingerprints will be all over it, and with the added truth that Lucas and I used to be a couple . . . Yeah, it's going to be bad."

"How can I help?"

"I don't think you can. I told Sheriff Allen everything I know, and according to Cheryl, Poppy was the one who bought the dagger yesterday."

"Maybe Poppy stabbed him. He seems to have a knack for getting on people's bad sides." Frannie winked as she offered me a hilarious finger gun.

I stroked my chin. "That doesn't make any sense. Lucas is extremely influential and drenched in money.

No one would be stupid enough to take out their own meal ticket. Not without some other reason."

Frannie looked dubious, and she shrugged. "If you say so. What's your next move?"

My shoulders drooped. "No idea. Maybe I'll head back to the manor and see if there's a snowball's chance in hell of convincing everyone I'm innocent."

"I'm here if you need anything."

Her kind words hit me hard. "Hey, I'm beyond sorry about my disgusting behavior. I know the dagger is cursed, but that's no excuse. You're my best friend, and I'm so embarrassed I spoke to you and treated you the way I did." I struggled to hold back tears. "Never again. I promise."

Frannie lifted her right fist and extended her pinky. "Pinky promise?"

I immediately hooked my pinky through hers and shook three times. "Pinky promise."

We hugged it out, cried a little, and laughed through the tears. "Wish me luck, Frannie."

She unlocked the door and rubbed my back as I exited. "Good luck, Syd."

As I made my way back to Moonlight Manor, I kept my speed five-below, assuming I'd see a patrol car. But the police vehicles were gone, and Lucas's car had already been towed by the time I passed the site of the murder. Driving alone on the moonlit road sent eerie chills down my spine.

Everything appeared in black and white, as the moon's glow reflected off the snowy road. Everything, except the motive behind this crime. The creepy dagger had been taken and now my ex-boyfriend was dead. He'd been left in the ditch by the side of the road. Who could have killed him?

As soon as I got the front door closed behind me, I yelled. "Sir Bogart? Velma? Norman? I have terrible news."

As I peeled off my hat, mittens, and jacket, the ghosts appeared one by one.

Sir Bogart leapt onto the settee and settled in.

Norman drifted forward, took my outerwear, and laid it on a chair.

Velma hovered nearby with a worried look on her face.

Rubbing my hand over my face, I exhaled loudly and stifled a sob. "Lucas is dead."

Bogey's relaxed pose immediately shifted to a tense crouch. He was ready to spring into action at a moment's notice. "When was this heinous deed committed?"

I described the roadside scene, and a single tear leaked from the corner of my eye.

Velma hurried forward and attempted to comfort me. She tried to pat my shoulder, but other than creating a bit of a chill, her actions didn't accomplish much. "I'm so sorry, miss. I know he were terrible and whatnot, but he didn't deserve that."

I nodded in agreement.

"Is there more, mistress?" Bogey's whiskers twitched.

"Yes. Sheriff Allen thinks the murder weapon might have been the dagger."

Sir Bogart's image paled, and a low hiss whispered through the room. "History has repeated itself. The sisters were right to lock that deadly blade away."

I dabbed at my eyes and then scowled at the feline. "What do you mean?"

"Edward Blodfyss murdered Reginald Williams. He stabbed the man in the back with the Dagger of Desire. The sisters carefully hid the clues and made the dagger disappear, but suspicion was ever present. The incident only added to the bitter feud between the two houses."

I gasped. "Are you saying that the dagger makes people commit murder? Why didn't you tell me sooner? You let me bandy it about. How could you—"

His tail twitched. "Mistress, if you'll please let me answer, I will explain."

"Sorry. But why did you let me keep a dagger that makes people murder others without telling me?"

"It's not in precisely those terms, mistress. The dagger is adept at uncovering evil, no matter how deeply it is buried. The seed must exist, but the dagger grows it at an unnatural pace. Without the deadly influence of the cursed blade, it is more than likely that Sir Edward would not have slain the Williams patriarch. Though, Sir Edward did not like him. Alas, men are quite eager to hide their immoral deeds behind the rumors of magic. Perhaps it is as your wise friend mentioned. Perhaps it was no fault of the dagger, but a mental instability that existed in Edward Blodfyss from the very start."

I winced as the truth of what Sir Bogart said settled in my heart. "I have to find that dagger, Bogey. Whatever it does, it's not good. You saw what happened to me, and I only had the thing for like a day. I still can't believe how rude I was to Frannie."

"Indeed."

I dabbed at another rivulet of tears as they journeyed down my cheeks. "What if someone else gets it? The dagger could cause more murders. Whoever has it now only had it a few hours, and Lucas is dead.

I have to get it back." A heavy silence hung in the room as we all adjusted to the weight of this burden.

Norman hovered closer to me. "Madam, shall I consult the grimoire for a possible magical alternative?"

"Is that wise?" I asked.

"Do you have another suggestion for locating the dagger, mistress? We suspect Poppy has it, and she is probably missing, but we have no other information than that."

My sigh echoed throughout the grand foyer. "Regardless, we're desperate, Norman. We have to find that dagger, and we have to lock it away forever. If there's any way to destroy a moon mark, I'd like to know. I don't want to risk someone finding it a hundred years from now and committing another murder. That blood would be on my head and on my hands. I can't have that."

Norman bowed and vanished.

I turned to the others. "I appreciate everyone's help. And all ideas are welcome. I mean it. But, um, I just need to be alone for a little while. It's been a super upsetting day already."

Velma curtsied. "I'll make you some tea, miss."

Bogey sauntered toward me and attempted to rub his regal head against my leg in an uncharacteristic show of support. "You are a good soul, Sydney Coleman. We will find a way forward—together."

I knelt down and did my best to stroke Sir Bogart's head and back. "Thank you," I whispered, trying to hold on to my composure a few minutes more.

Quietly, Sir Bogart disappeared from the room without the loud pop that normally followed.

After sharing the news with everyone at Moonlight Manor, I strode directly into the drawing room, plopped down on the hearth in front of a roaring fire lit by my thoughtful butler, and sobbed as hard as I ever had.

The tears weren't for me. The tears weren't for Lucas.

They were for everything I'd lost. The years I'd spent being someone I didn't want to be, the concessions I'd made to stay relevant in Lucas Aconite's life, and the horrible sight of my ex-boyfriend, lifeless in his luxury car. As much as I didn't like who he'd chosen to be as a person, I wouldn't have wished that on him. Never in a million years. He hadn't deserved that.

It was typical to repaint memories either rosy or dark, but the truth was, life with Lucas wasn't all bad. He had a hidden romantic streak. For our first date, he'd rented an entire restaurant so the two of us could have a private dinner without interruptions from his rivals or my fans, it touched me. It had been a rich boy flex, sure, but it had been one of the sweetest things anyone had done for me.

Time was the most valuable thing he possessed, and to think that he would give me an entire night—well, it made me think he was a better person than he actually was.

Now he was gone. Struck down in his prime by a jealous rival. I couldn't believe Kenny Holt would actually murder someone. The man was larger-than-life, and he spent most of his time, energy, and money pumping up his own ego. He struck me as a blowhard. One of those guys whose bark was always worse than his bite. But I supposed jealousy, rage, and humiliation could do strange things to a person.

What was I supposed to do now? Should I call the agency? Maybe I should call Lucas's parents. I didn't know them well, but we had spent two Thanksgivings and one Christmas with them. Granted, each of those visits was only a few hours, but I did know them. I'd met them at least.

No. I pushed the idea away. Sheriff Allen would certainly have her deputies contacting next of kin, and I was sure there were lawyers ready to dive into action the second news of Lucas Aconite's death hit the streets.

There was nothing for me to do. Unless sitting in my mansion, crying, and hoping I could prove my innocence counted, because right now that was the only thing I could do.

My head was swimming with memories—good and bad.

But when the doorbell chimed, no light shone in the sky, and I wasn't sure how much time had passed. I hoped it would be Sheriff Allen telling me this had all been a bad dream.

Making my way into the grand foyer, I swiped the tears from my face and took a few deep breaths before answering the door. "Deputy Johnson, how can I help you?"

Joe Johnson stood under the porch light in his official uniform, and I knew this wasn't a social visit. He held a piece of paper out and looked down at his boots. "I'm awful sorry, Sydney. I have a warrant to search the premises."

"Search Moonlight Manor? For what?"

He gestured to the warrant in my hand. "It's all in there. We're searching for the murder weapon. It wasn't left at the crime scene."

I gasped, wrinkled up the warrant, and threw it

on the ground. "Joe. I didn't do this. I don't have a murder weapon in my home because I didn't murder anyone."

He took off his hat, held it to his chest, and shook his head. "Like I said, I'm awful sorry. But if I don't conduct the search, Sheriff Allen will send someone else. I'll be real respectful, Sydney. You have my word."

I stepped back, flinging the door so hard the edge slammed against the wall behind it. "Fine. Come on in, Deputy Johnson. If you want to waste your time, it's fine by me."

He headed toward the back of the manor, and I followed. He turned and put up a hand. "I'm sorry. I'll need you to remain in that front room. Please don't cause any trouble, Sydney."

A shocked expression gripped my face, and I crossed my arms firmly over my chest. "Me? I'm not the one causing trouble. You're basically accusing me of murder. That's the trouble. Decent people who report crimes are treated like criminals."

He shook his head and continued as though I hadn't spoken. "I'm going to start in the ballroom, since that's where the majority of the people were."

"Fine." I marched to the drawing room and sat on the ottoman in front of the fire, angrily tapping my toes. I crossed my arms and stewed over the latest development. I'd wanted to report the dagger missing, and I'd come across a dead body. Calling it in had been a mistake.

Far sooner than I would've liked, Deputy Johnson returned to the drawing room with the dagger in an evidence bag. "I'll be taking this into the station, Miss Coleman. If the lab confirms it's the murder weapon, I'm afraid I'll have to place you under arrest." His eyes avoided mine. "Please don't leave town, miss."

All I could manage was a curt nod. If I opened my mouth, I'd either scream or cry.

17

After Deputy Johnson discovered the weapon in my home, the very real possibility of a murder charge lit a fire under my rear end. How could the dagger have been returned to my home? Who had brought it back to Moonlight Manor?

Marching upstairs, I took a quick shower and attempted to cover the bags under my eyes with some clever contouring makeup. The sun was peeking over the horizon and it was time to make an actual plan.

All good plans start with coffee. I brewed a strong pot and got to work. Perhaps Norman had found something in the grimoire. I would need to check in with him soon as well.

I scrolled through my phone and found an old

contact at the Aconite Agency that I hoped I could still trust. Selecting the number, I waited as the line rang three times.

"Hello?"

"Teresa? It's Sydney Coleman." She was surprised to hear from me, couldn't believe it was really me, and wondered what I'd been up to.

Clearly, news of their leader's death hadn't reached the masses. Rather than be the leak, I thought it might work in my favor to play the jealous ex-girlfriend. "Hey, I totally understand if you don't want to get involved, but who is this Poppy that Lucas is seeing?"

Teresa pretended to care about my feelings and said a bunch of negative things about Poppy. But I needed dependable information, not a gossip sesh. "Thanks, Teresa. It's good to know that I have at least one friend at the agency. But I seriously wanted to find out more about her. Like when she got hired, what department she works in, and how long she and Lucas have been together."

When I learned the truth, I was more terrified than comforted.

Poppy Peters was a reporter for a hot new e-zine. She got involved with Lucas when she started interviewing him for a huge article titled The Sexiest Man in Advertising. Of course he would've agreed. That kind of clickbait title would feed directly into his hungry ego.

Would Poppy have created her own story? Someone had to know where Poppy Peters was. At least I had her whole name now. Maybe a few more calls would accomplish something. I grimaced. I'd at least have a name when Sheriff Allen came to arrest me for real and maybe Poppy would call me for my side of the story when the prison bars clanged shut.

Imagining the metallic sound of the metal doors closing made me shudder. I needed to talk to some big time social media influencers. If anyone knew about a hot new e-zine, it was the blogosphere royalty.

I fired off carefully worded text messages to the top three social media golden girls in my roster. Two of them replied almost instantly. Neither of them had heard of Poppy Peters or her e-zine. But they both agreed that Lucas was the sexiest man in advertising. I thanked them for the intel and quickly searched their feeds for something they'd recently posted that I could comment on.

A disturbing picture was shaping up. Lucas had been sucked into Poppy Peters's web with complete and total falsehoods. Had Poppy Peters even been a real person? Or something completely fabricated? If my girls didn't know about her, it didn't bode well. I conducted my own online search and quickly confirmed no such person or e-zine existed.

So, if she wasn't Poppy Peters and she wasn't a reporter. Who was she?

I set my phone down and accepted a coffee refill from Velma. Sipping it carefully as I planned my next move. Who would have it out for Lucas? And could I conduct an investigation with only a laptop and a cell phone?

When the text notification pinged on my phone, it shocked me to see a reply from the reigning queen of viral videos. She didn't waste any time on niceties or falsehoods about how great it was to hear from me. She cut straight to the heart of the matter.

Poppy Peters was a complete and total fraud. She wasn't a reporter or even someone working in the ad business. Poppy Peters was a high-end escort for hire. What? Why would Lucas do that?

The news shocked me so hard, I typed my reply without thinking. It was too emotional and lacked the polish of my former life.

And it was too late to un-send it. *Fiddlesticks.*

Instead of wallowing in regret, I dialed Frannie and spilled the new information with the phone on speaker so I could warm my hands around my cup of java.

"Syd, you have to call Sheriff Allen and give her this information. If they're looking for someone named Poppy Peters, they're never going to find her. It's just some bogus name, some alias. Did you find any pictures of her online?"

"No. That was my first confirmation that Lucas had been hoodwinked. He must have a picture of her on his phone, though. I saw Sheriff Allen slip his phone into an evidence bag at the scene."

Frannie mumbled her agreement. "But they won't be able to unlock the phone. She can only see the recent calls, because they were on the splash screen. The deputies won't be able to access the photos without his password."

The comment gave me pause, and my voice grew soft. "His password used to be my birthdate. Back when he swore we had no secrets from each other. But once he started cheating on me, I'm sure he changed it."

She disagreed. "Don't be so sure. I really think you should call Sheriff Allen."

"All right. I'll call her. But can you come out to the manor? I definitely don't want to be alone when I get arrested."

I could hear the smile in Frannie's voice when she replied. "Of course. I just have to throw a couple batches of brioche dough in the fridge to proof, and I'll be on my way. Should I grab some breakfast, or bring more quiches?"

"Grab something for yourself. I don't have an appetite."

Frannie groaned loudly. "Who's not hungry? Is this curly-haired, kind-hearted Sydney or is this that colossal B-word Sydney?"

My breath caught in my throat, but only for a half a second. "Yep, I had that coming. But it's just simple country girl, Sydney. It was really awful yesterday. I don't want to rehash the details, but—"

"Say no more. I'll see you when I see you."

When my thoughtful friend finally arrived, I hadn't moved from my seat in the drawing room. Maybe I was still in shock over Lucas, but as soon as I caught a whiff of her scrumptious bacon and onion mini quiche, I regretted turning down any food. I took a deep breath in.

Frannie let herself in, glanced at my expression, and giggled. "Don't worry, I brought enough for two. Let's head into the kitchen and devour this deliciousness while we plan our next move."

She didn't have to summon me twice, and I

followed her to the kitchen table. When she'd finished her share, I was about halfway through mine when a frantic pounding on the mudroom door gave us both a fright.

Frannie darted toward the stove, picked up a frying pan, and led the way to the mudroom. "Get your phone ready to call 911. I don't know how accurate I am with this thing, but I doubt I'll get two chances."

When we pulled the door open, it was disorienting to see the tear-stained face of Candi. She wore knee-high white faux fur boots, a fur miniskirt, and a faux fur bandeau top. Despite the warmth of the parts that were covered, a great deal of Candi was exposed to the elements. And early winter Maine wasn't kind to exposed parts.

I pushed around Frannie and hooked my arm around Candi. "Oh, my. Come in. You must be freezing."

She lurched forward and supported herself on my shoulders. "Oh, Sydney. I didn't know where else to go. I followed your tracks along the trail, and here I am."

Frannie led the way back into the kitchen and put the kettle on while I fetched a blanket for our new guest. When I returned, I guided her to an open seat.

As I tucked the blanket around her, I rubbed it on her skin to help warm her up as quickly as possible. "Candi, what happened? Why are you so upset?"

"Sydney, he's replacing me," she cried. "I gave that man everything. I work out three hours a day to stay in shape. It's not easy for a woman in her forties to keep up this figure."

Frannie and I exchanged wide-eyed gazes. Forties? Candi was doing an amazing job. Maybe I hadn't looked close enough earlier, but I'd definitely placed her under thirty. "Guys like Kenny are always going to be trading in for a younger model. It's not your fault, Candi. You look amazing."

She placed a hand on her concave stomach and moaned. "Are you sure? I think maybe I'm getting fat."

Frannie could no longer contain herself. She laughed openly. "Candi. You're wrong. You look amazing, and this Kenny person is an idiot. But why would he bring you all the way up to Maine and then break up with you?"

"I don't know. It was so weird. But when Poppy showed up at the Mercedes, he told me to get out." She touched the sapphire pendant hanging around her neck. "He just got me this present, and he kicks me out into the snow like little orphan Oliver."

Candi had clearly confused her orphan stories, but that wasn't really the point. "Did you say *Poppy?*" I asked, widening my eyes. "Kenny got rid of you for *her?*"

She wiped a finger under each of her eyes and sniffled. "I know. Right?"

I glanced at Frannie and grinned. "That's the connection. Poppy met Kenny through her escort services, and he hired her to buy the dagger. That way, he thought it wouldn't get traced back to him."

Candi's face paled. "Escort? Kenny is cheating on me with a hooker?"

"Um, no. I don't think so. Maybe he just hired Poppy to do this job. We don't know if he was actually sleeping with her."

"What job?" Candi's wail turned into a sob, and Frannie handed her a wad of paper towels. Candi scrubbed it over her splotchy face.

Frannie frowned. "But how would he know about it? He hadn't seen it before the preview day. Didn't you say she," she pointed at the woman in question, "dragged it out of your room?"

I met Frannie's gaze over Candi's head. "I'm not sure. Maybe he recognized Poppy and made a call. I can't be sure, but I need to find out."

Frannie patted Candi's convulsing back. "What do you mean?"

"If Poppy is over there right now, I think we should sneak over and try to get some pictures of them together. Then we'll really have something to give Sheriff Allen. And she'll have to take me off the suspect list."

The glamazon blew her nose like a foghorn, and I covered my mouth to keep from laughing.

"You're a suspect, Sydney? In what?" Candi asked.

"Lucas Aconite was murdered this morning." It hurt every time I had to say it out loud.

"OMG. Kenny was so mad about that furniture. He swore he was gonna kill Lucas. I just can't believe Kenny would do that." And she was sobbing again.

"Candi. You stay here and make yourself at home. Frannie and I can sneak back over to the motorhome and see if we can get some pictures of Poppy and Kenny together."

She gasped. "Like *together* together? Do you think they're sleeping together?"

I couldn't be sure what I thought. But I wasn't about to send her into another shame spiral. "I don't think so. I meant more like pictures of them plotting and planning. Maybe Poppy came back to try and get more money from Kenny. She's the only one who knows about buying the dagger for him. If he really did kill Lucas, she might be in danger."

Candi wiped her nose and got to her feet. She towered above Frannie and me. "Give me a coat or something. I'm coming with you. If Kenny killed someone, I'm going to make sure he pays for it. If he's cheating on me, he's going to be the next victim."

Wow. Remind me not to cross a half-starved gold digger again, if I can help it. Perpetual hunger could make people extremely angry. And determined, too.

A few minutes later, Candi looped a belt around her middle, but I didn't have a coat that would close over Candi's buxom bosom. At least I was able to find a long coat that covered most of her bare legs.

We all had our phones, and we marched through the snow toward the condemned Williams estate.

18

Candi's height proved quite an advantage outside the motorhome, as most of the windows were several feet off the ground. I recorded the conversation on my phone, while Candi took pictures on hers, in between sniffling over the loss of "her Kenny."

Inside the travel trailer, Kenny and Poppy weren't exactly arguing, but they were having a heated discussion about the murder and Poppy planting the dagger in my mansion. Within two minutes, I had Poppy confessing to stabbing Lucas and then waiting until I'd gone out to plant the dagger back at Moonlight Manor.

Pressing my lips together, I shook my finger at the trailer. It would be too risky to play back the recording, to see if the microphone was able to catch the muffled conversation. But three eyewitness accounts plus the reel of photos on Candi's phone should be enough.

I gestured for us to leave, and Candi tripped over the cable running from the generator. She fell hard and yelped. The sound echoed over the snow. Frantic thumping sounded inside the trailer.

Seconds later, the door flew open, and Poppy trained her gun on the intruders. To be clear, that would be us. She stepped out with Kenny close behind.

"Hand over your phones." She waved the gun threateningly, and her shaved head made her that much more intimidating. "Now."

Frannie and I handed them over, but not Candi.

"Please don't sh-sh-shoot, Poppy. I lost my phone when I fell in the snow. You just shoved me out of the trailer and into the c-c-c-cold. It's long gone." Candi sobbed and hid her face in her hands. "You know how clumsy I am, Kenny."

If Candi thought her aging Lothario would jump to her rescue, she had sorely misread the room. Kenny gave her a disgusted look and shook his head. He didn't come to her rescue.

Poppy glanced at Kenny, and her upper lip curled.

When she turned back to Candi, she scoffed and snarled. "Get inside."

We tripped over each other to comply with the request of our gun-toting captor, and we entered the motorhome single-file up the stairs.

"Into the sauna," Poppy commanded next, barking the order over Candi's whimpers.

As soon as the three of us stepped inside the sauna, Poppy wedged a chair up against the door, cranked the heat, and left with Kenny. Then she stuck her face in the little window and waved.

Two of us peeled off our coats and boots and sighed. It didn't feel that hot. Maybe we'd be okay for a while. If the three of us worked together, we could probably knock that chair loose.

The thought of steaming to death made my skin crawl, and in a moment of vanity I imagined how frizzy my hair would be when they discovered my body. I'd be a veritable bobblehead doll.

Candi, oddly silent, shrugged off the borrowed coat and smiled. She tucked herself into the corner of the sauna.

"You're remarkably happy about the circumstances, Candi. Do you know some secret way out of this sauna?"

Her hand disappeared into her cavernous

cleavage and returned a moment later with her phone. "So maybe I didn't lose it in the snow."

Frannie and I clapped in unison. "Candi, you're a genius," I whooped.

She blushed and handed me the phone. "No one's ever called me that before."

"Well, it's true," Frannie added.

"Oh, stop that." She pointed to the phone. "You should probably call the sheriff."

"I should absolutely call the sheriff," I agreed.

As soon as Sheriff Allen got on the line, I explained about our predicament and gave her the backstory on Poppy and Kenny. I also mentioned we recorded their conversation, but I added that—oops—Poppy took my phone. Candi still had pictures, though.

For a moment, Sheriff Allen remained quiet. "Go on."

"Poppy was the one who stashed the dagger in the piano bench, where Deputy Johnson later found it. She's the one who murdered L-Lucas." His name came out in a hiccup. I didn't think I would ever get used to saying that my ex had been murdered.

On the other end of the line, Sheriff Allen sighed. "Very well. If everything you say is true, Miss Coleman, you'll be cleared of any wrongdoing. We'll work to corroborate your story, and I'll send Joe out there to get you all out of the sauna."

"What about Kenny and Poppy?" I asked. "They'll escape."

"Don't you worry. The rest of the deputies and I will take care of those two," she said. "Now, what kind of car does Kenny drive?"

I lowered the phone. "The sheriff wants to know what kind of car Kenny drives?"

Candi tapped her long fingernail against her gleaming white teeth. "Um, let me think."

The longer the thinking went on, the more I thought we'd have to give up hope.

But then, all at once, she came through. "He has a late-model black Range Rover SUV."

Raising my eyebrows, I nodded. "Nicely done." After relaying that information to Sheriff Allen, the call ended, and we waited for Joe to show up.

I wiped the moisture from Candi's phone screen by rubbing it against my pant leg. "Do you think he'll get here in time?" I glanced around the small room. "I'm not sure how much of this I can take."

Sweat beaded on Frannie's upper lip. "I'm sure we'll be fine."

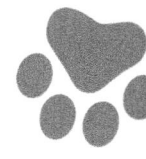

19

The temperature inside the sauna rose higher, and Candi instructed us all to take shallow breaths and remain as motionless as possible. "You don't want to get that hot air too deep into your lungs. Try to breathe through your nose, and remain calm. Help is on the way. We're all gonna be just fine."

At least I'd have plenty of time to reflect on how badly I misjudged Candi. I'd heard the saying many times, "don't judge a book by its cover," but in the world of social media influencing, that was the only way to judge anything. My snap judgments had garnered me several advertising awards, but in the game of friendship, it was obvious I had a lot to learn.

By the time Joe found us, our situation had turned dire. We were drenched in sweat and leaning against the walls of the sauna, panting. The thing should have had a fail-safe.

If Candi hadn't thought to hide her phone and play off her clumsiness, our story would have had a very different ending. It might have had a different ending if she hadn't been there to coach us on how to keep cooler.

A thump-thump-thump roused us. "You in there, Sydney? Frannie?"

"Joe? Is that you?" I rasped. Frannie didn't answer.

"Hurry," Candi called.

When the door of the sauna opened and the cold air rushed in, I thought I might finally know what it felt like when an angel got its wings.

I helped Frannie to her feet, and we all stumbled out of the sweatbox and thanked Joe profusely. He helped us into the back of his cruiser and drove the short distance to Moonlight Manor. We cracked the windows, basking in the cold Maine air.

It wasn't long before something unexpected caught my attention.

I banged on the back of Joe's seat. "Turn it up."

"What?"

"The police radio, turn it up," I repeated. "Something's going on."

He obliged, and the information coming over the police radio shocked us all.

We leaned toward the front seat, each one of us almost holding our breaths. There was a standoff on the highway. Poppy fired on the deputies, and the Sheriff returned fire. One of the perpetrators had been shot in the shoulder, but they didn't say which one.

Candi cried. "I'm sure it's Kenny. He's not cut out for this kind of thing. He might be a New York City boy, but he's the kind of New York City boy that buys tickets to Broadway, and enjoys six-course dinners at fancy restaurants. My Kenny's not a gangster."

By the time we reached the manor, the perpetrators were in custody, and Kenny Holt was being treated on-site for a bullet graze to his left shoulder. Deputy Johnson escorted us into the manor and took our statements.

Not long after Deputy Johnson left Moonlight Manor, Sheriff Allen called to explain how Poppy had gotten involved in the murder of Lucas Aconite. Fortunately for all of us, Sheriff Allen felt a great deal of guilt for accusing me of yet another murder, and to make up for it, she dished everything they'd discovered since catching Kenny and Poppy. I switched to speaker phone, and we all huddled around it.

At least five years ago, Lucas had severely humiliated Poppy in front of several senior ad executives. I remembered a few of those incidents but struggled to place her. Poppy had been fired without cause, but apparently Lucas had gone the extra mile and blackballed her. She couldn't get hired anywhere. Eventually, she lost a bunch of weight, shaved her head, and started working as an escort under the name Poppy.

When she met Kenny through a legitimate job, escorting him to an awards banquet, they somehow discovered a shared hatred of Lucas Aconite.

As Candi had mentioned, Kenny was no gangster. But his pride was sufficiently wounded by Lucas often enough to allow him to bankroll Poppy's plan. Once she had concocted the cover story and gotten Lucas to agree to The Sexiest Man in Advertising interview, she'd shown him an article about *my* antique sale. Lucas had asked her to also accompany him to a weekend of antique-hunting in Maine, and she had agreed.

Sheriff Allen admitted that Poppy had probably recognized my name and known me as Lucas's ex-girlfriend. In this way, Poppy engineered a trip into a less populated corner of the world with Lucas.

She had originally intended to shoot Lucas in Maine and dump his body in the woods. But according to Sheriff Allen, once Poppy met me during the auction preview and Lucas had complained I was his ex-girlfriend, the one he hired Poppy to make jealous, she was eager to frame me for the crime. That's when she and Kenny cooked up the idea to use something from my manor as the murder weapon. Once they found the dagger on the sales tables at the antique auction, Poppy had what she needed.

It remained unclear whether Candi's fascination with the dagger on preview day had led the culprits to choose it as the murder weapon, but it ultimately didn't matter.

I took in a sharp breath. What a series of unfortunate events that had led to Lucas's death. When the ugly-hearted people started circling, they didn't have a chance to withstand the conniving blade. What Sir Bogart said about the dagger sensing a seed of malice was obviously true in Poppy's case. Once she had the dangerous weapon, it was simple to convince her to complete her horrible plot.

Sheriff Allen was sorry to report that Kenny already had a team of lawyers at the station and was looking for any deal available. He blamed everything on Poppy, and even though it wasn't fair, the sheriff assured me that his money would set him free. While Poppy had nobody.

Candi was ecstatic and already talking about meeting "her Kenny" the moment he was free. There was no accounting for taste.

20

The Dagger of Desire had to remain in police custody until the trial was complete. But Sir Bogart and I had Sheriff Allen's personal assurance that it would be returned to me when the proceedings were over.

Norman hadn't uncovered a way to remove the moon mark on the shelf in the hidden room, but he had discovered some delicious-sounding Yule recipes and an oddly appropriate winter solstice blessing in the grimoire.

For the second time in as many months, I'd managed to avoid being charged with a murder I hadn't committed, and I hoped it would be the last time I was on the short list of suspects for anything like that. Though, I had a feeling Moonlight Manor probably had more surprises in store.

With all the stress of preparing for the huge estate sale, and then the deadly dagger drama—I'd nearly forgotten it was Christmas. So many people had made sacrifices to help me stay in Moonlight Manor, and in Misty Meadows. I wanted to thank them with a proper feast.

Frannie promised to help me cook the holiday meal. In reality, that meant she'd cook the meal and I'd focus on organizing the event, decorating the manor, and inviting the guests. As we prepared, Velma was beside herself at the prospect of entertaining. She kept saying over and over how much she'd missed it.

My list included Joe and Cheryl, Davis and his father Paul, Candi, Craig, Mia, Sheriff Allen, and Augusta Adams. My only "no" was Augusta. She had grandchildren in Vermont that she would spend the holidays with. It was a surprise to receive a "yes" from the sheriff, but that seemed like a good sign. Maybe Haley had learned enough about me to officially remove me from future suspect lists.

As I gazed at the massive table in the formal dining room, it was the first time my antique china, polished silver, and crystal stemware seemed appropriate. Norman had gone out of his way to set the dining room to spectacular perfection. He and Velma had even created three gorgeous centerpieces, with candles and holly they must've found in some storage closet.

Davis Martin had harvested pine boughs from the property and helped me secure them on the mantles and over the entryway. Everything looked incredible, and I was sure the manor couldn't look any more spectacular . . . However, Craig shocked my socks off when he arrived with a massive pine tree hanging out of the bed of his brand new four-wheel-drive truck.

He hurried onto the porch, and I opened the door before he could knock.

"Is Davis here?" he called.

"Here," Davis called, trotting through the grand foyer.

I beamed at my handyman-turned-friend. "Davis, I think Craig needs some help bringing in the tree."

A tree. All the wonderful memories of mulled cider and Christmas morning with my brothers came flooding back. I'd never had a Christmas tree the whole time I'd been in New York City, and it pleased me so much now. As Craig and Davis went out to bring the holiday icon inside, I studied the shining faces of my friends.

This camaraderie was what my life had been lacking. Jet-setting to far off islands and sipping fruity drinks on a private beach had its perks, but the old-fashioned cheer of "winging it" with close friends filled my heart with hope and happiness.

Maybe next year I'd invite my family to join me at the manor. I hadn't seen them in years. It would be healing to clear the air and rebuild those relationships. Heck, why wait a year? No need to use a holiday as an excuse. I'd call them each tomorrow and make amends. An open invitation sounded like a good start. I grinned. Wouldn't my family be shocked to find out I owned Moonlight Manor and now lived in small-town Maine? Would wonders never cease?

As Davis and Craig wrestled old Tannenbaum from the truck, Velma whispered in my ear. "There are crates of decorations in the attic, miss. Should Norman and I bring them down?"

A smile spread across my face. "What a wonderful idea," I whispered behind my hand, careful to keep my eyes on the ground, just in case someone might be watching me converse with the air. "Just bring them down to the second floor, though. I don't want to frighten anyone."

"Yes, miss."

Time to check on dinner, so I bustled into the kitchen.

Frannie, Mia, and Haley had everything humming. There was a ham and a goose in the oven, gravy bubbling on the stove, pull-apart rolls cooling on the island, and innumerable empty serving bowls waiting for an array of luscious side dishes. The best part? I hadn't made any of it, a fact all of my friends would probably appreciate.

I took a deep breath. "Mmmm. It smells amazing in here. Haley, don't take this the wrong way, but I think you're an even better cook than a sheriff."

Luckily, Haley took my words as a compliment, and we all shared a heartfelt chuckle.

Haley stepped toward me and lowered her voice, "Thanks for including me, Sydney. I'm sorry about the whole suspect thing with Lucas Aconite's murder, but I'm sure you understand."

The truth was I didn't really understand. Nobody had ever accused me of murder before, least of all twice. But tonight was about building a bright future, not holding grudges.

I wanted Haley as my friend rather than my sheriff, so I circled an arm around her shoulders and whispered, "Sir Bogart insisted."

She blushed, and I gave her a squeeze.

Haley nodded appreciatively and poured us each a splash of wine from the open bottle on the counter. "Here's to old friends, new friends, and fresh starts."

We clinked our glasses, and I offered a conspiratorial wink.

Davis and Craig burst into the kitchen and reported that the massive tree was in position in the ballroom, and I caught sight of the stack of boxes at the top of the stairs on the second level. I waved to Joe and Cheryl as they hung up their coats. "Hey, can you guys bring down the decorations? Those crates, right up there."

Frannie shooed us all out of "her" kitchen. "That enormous tree isn't going to decorate itself. I'll hold down the fort in here, and the rest of you get busy making Christmas."

Cheryl and Joe carried the decorations into the ballroom.

"Don't you trip, Joe. Your box probably has all the breakable ornaments in it," she teased.

Joe winked at Cheryl and then at me. His cheeks had turned rosy from the warmth inside the manor and the extra thick Christmas sweater he wore. Or maybe he'd already had a glass of Christmas cheer. I couldn't be sure, I decided with a grin.

They placed the crates near the tree, and I opened every single one. Each box contained a time capsule of trinkets. Even Davis stopped his horseplay with Joe when we opened the box of delicate glass pinecones and faux birds crafted from real feathers. Mia took charge of the paper butterflies, and I hung the fragile bundles of cinnamon sticks and dried herbs.

The decision to leave the real candles off the tree was unanimous. We wanted a festive dinner party, not a reason to call the fire department. Haley breathed a visible sigh of relief when we set that crate aside.

We opted for the bubbler lights, which must have belonged to Beatrix, and loads of tinsel. When it came time to place the tarnished glass star atop the giant pine, I sadly assumed we'd have to skip that part of the holiday tradition. But then Davis disappeared and returned with a huge ladder.

"Come on, Syd. You should be the one to place the star." Davis offered me one hand, and held the ladder with the other.

I didn't exactly have a fear of heights, but I wasn't crazy about climbing a rickety ladder in front of a room full of people. When I looked up into his warm gaze, my fear melted. Taking his outstretched hand, I started up the ladder. Mia handed me the star, and a surge of emotion forced me to stop and steady myself.

"I'm going to have to lean way out." My voice shook.

"Don't worry. I've got a great hold on this." Davis grinned. "And if you fall, I'll catch you. I used to catch the cheerleaders during the half-time show. Right, Joe?"

Joe chuckled wickedly. "And *after* the game, if I recall correctly, Squatchy."

Cheryl punched him. "It's Christmas. Behave yourself, Joseph Johnson."

Glancing down, I had to smile. Davis was holding the base of the ladder so tightly a tow truck couldn't have pulled it from his grasp. I used everything I'd learned in my three weeks of ballet classes and leaned precariously toward the treetop.

Velma and Norman appeared—for my eyes only—and offered me their glowing support as I teetered toward the highest bough.

I whispered my thanks and admired our group effort. "Merry Christmas."

"Happy Christmas, madam."

"Merry Christmas, miss."

As soon as the star settled into place, cheers and

applause echoed up from the crowd, and Craig plugged in the bubble lights.

The ladder tilted, and I let out a frightened yelp. "You better not be clapping, Davis."

He grinned up at me and winked. "I've got you, Sydney."

My heart stuttered. Maybe he was right . . . He did have me—in more ways than one. But I'd save the swooning for later, when we were alone. I wasn't sure I wanted an audience for my first romantic spark in Moonlight Manor. Besides, keeping my wits and my balance were crucial to a safe descent, and if I thought too much about Davis, I wouldn't be able to keep either.

Sir Bogart floated into the ballroom and joined Norman and Velma. The trio smiled proudly at my efforts.

"Supper is served," Frannie called from the dining room and the group hurried toward the inviting aromas.

Davis took my hand when I reached the bottom of the ladder. "See? Safe and sound."

I let my tiny hand rest in his large one, and smiled up into his twinkling green eyes. "Thanks, Squatchy."

He chuckled and escorted me to the head of the

table. Frannie sat opposite me, ready to hustle off to the kitchen at a moment's notice.

"Thank you all for coming tonight. I'd like to read a special winter solstice blessing that has been in the Blodfyss family for over one hundred years."

Outside, the earth sleeps in an icy fog,
bare oak offers mistletoe to the knife.
Inside we give thanks for a warm yule-log,
burning your acorn brings wishes to life.
The sun must sleep for its lengthy, dark night,
the world awaits the chance to be reborn.
Cinnamon and clove—the wassails sweet light,
we toast family and new oaths are sworn.
We steal a kiss under the mistletoe,
and sing as we dance the solstice along.
A gift of ornaments passed in fire's glow,
and chills chased away by the warmth of song.
Cheers signal the start of the solar feast,
longest night fades—golden sun in the East.

Raising my glass, I glanced across the gathered faces and smiled. "Cheers."

"Cheers," echoed from those gathered, and Frannie carved the goose. Everyone picked up a dish of something and passed it around the beautiful table, and we piled food high on our plates. The meal was unforgettable and the company unmatched.

My first Christmas in Moonlight Manor, and I was surrounded by true friends and the genuine spirit—or should I say spirits—of the season.

We were truly blessed, one and all.

A SNEAK PEEK FROM TRIXIE
FROM FRIES AND ALIBIS

A gift that's too good to be true. A murder she didn't commit. A barista in a latte trouble…

Mitzy Moon believes she's an orphan, so she's dumbstruck when a special delivery to her low-rent apartment reveals a family. But her shock turns to awe when she discovers her grandmother left her a fortune and a bookshop of rare tomes brimming with magic.

No sooner does she set foot in the quirky village of Pin Cherry Harbor to claim her inheritance, than the handsome sheriff catches her standing over a corpse. Desperate to prove her innocence, she's forced to accept help from her granny's entitled cat and a spirit from beyond the grave.

Can Mitzy and her otherworldly helpers uncover the real killer before the long, sexy arm of the law hauls her to jail?

Fries and Alibis is the first book in the hilarious paranormal cozy mystery series, Mitzy Moon Mysteries. If you like amateur sleuths, small town intrigue, and a dash of the supernatural, then you'll love Trixie Silvertale's twisty whodunit.

<u>Buy Fries and Alibis to serve up the guilty today!</u>

You can also turn the page to read the first chapter…

READ THIS HILARIOUS SNEAK PEEK

Well, I'll be a monkey's uncle! You actually can't miss it. Right on the corner of Main and First. I lean back and shade my eyes against the mid-morning sun. "Wow!" I look around to see if anyone heard my exclamation, but the streets are devoid of walkers, and the old truck sputtering down the road can't hear a thing.

I walk down the side of the massive three-story brick building and run my hand along the rough red-brown surface. I catch my breath as I come face to face with the "great lake" mentioned in the documents, which provided much-needed entertainment on the bus. "Wow!" I say again.

I've never seen this much water in my entire life. The sheer volume is obscene. A flash flood in the desert during the brief monsoon season is a dripping faucet compared to this lush, liquid paradise. The sun sparkles off the water, birds swoop and dive overhead, the cool breeze flutters my hair, and—

"Hey there, you gonna open up or not?"

I swallow my awe and turn to see one of the pairs of eyes from the diner posted up outside my bookshop. I guess I'm gonna open.

I slip the chain with the key over my head as I walk toward my first customer. "I'm Mitzy. What's your name?" The woman looks about fifty or sixty. I'm not that great at guessing people's ages. Her black denim pants, Styx T-shirt, and biker boots say fifty-ish, but her severe grey pixie and lined face whisper an older tale.

"I didn't come for chit-chat, girlie. Are ya opening or not?"

So much for Midwestern charm.

The eight-foot solid wood door that bars my entry to the bookshop is a work of art. I don't have time to inspect the careful craftsmanship that adorns the massive piece with delicate and detailed carving—there is too much sighing and foot tapping behind me. I run my fingers along the edge opposite the hefty iron hinges and locate the cleverly concealed opening that contains the "plug." Yes, I did learn how to pick locks from a delinquent older foster brother. But even he couldn't have popped this cherry. His gross term, not mine. I slide my triangular key into the lock and turn. I don't hear a click so much as I "feel" the lock open. I actually think I felt the whole store awaken. And I realize that sounds as weird as it —well, sounds.

I pull the heavy, ornate door open and have to physically arm-bar the patron from entering before me. It's my shop. I want to be the first to walk in.

No Chit-chat exhales loudly.

I feel around on the left and right for the light switches. Nothing. Goose egg. Nada.

"Oh for cryin' out loud," exclaims No Chit-chat as she bustles past me and disappears into the store.

I gaze around in the dust-filtered window-light and breathe in the scent of worlds. I imagine a short film that will take place within—

LIGHTS.

A massive chandelier flashes to life above me and I gasp.

I crane my neck to take in the impossibly voluminous space. The building did not look anywhere near this large from the outside. There are three stories of bookshelves. All the way from the richly carpeted floor to the gleaming tin-plated ceiling.

A balcony curves from one side of the second floor to the other, passing through a lovely loft/mezzanine in the back.

I drop my bags to the floor and hop-step over the "No Admittance" chain, run up the wrought-iron circular staircase to the open-plan second floor, and take in the mesmerizing view back toward the rows of slumped-glass windows. Dust floating in the air seems to ride on a gentle breeze down to the bookcases in their thick, stoic rows on the first floor.

"You need me to run to the bank and get the drawer money?"

Oh crap, I completely forgot about my customer. I hurry down the stairs, trip a little, catch myself on the railing, stumble over my bags, and skitter to a halt in front of No Chit-chat. "Why would I need drawer money? And why would I send you to get it if I did, Mrs.—?"

"Nope. No 'Mrs.' Never wrapped that noose around my neck. Everybody calls me 'Twiggy.'"

Twiggy. Hmmm. Now that would be the perfect name for Fat Carol. "All right. Can I help you find something today, Twiggy?"

"You can't even find the lights, doll. And to answer one of your many earlier questions, you need drawer money to put in the cash register." She puts up a finger, capped by a close-clipped nail, to shush me and continues, "You send me to get it 'cuz I been workin' part-time for your Grams during high season since she had this old brewery converted into a bookstore."

I glance around the utterly empty bookshop and nod and smile. "Well, how is it that you have access to my grandmother's—rather—my bank account?"

"Are you always this thick, or did you hit your head when you tackled the sheriff?"

I clench my jaw to prevent a stream of unladylike phrases from spilling out of my beautiful mouth. "Humor me," I manage to say.

"Tilly's been the teller at the bank practically since the money came by stagecoach. She knows me.

She knew your Grams. I walk in, ask for the drawer money, and she hands it over." Twiggy shakes her head like she's ashamed of me. "If I went in there and ask Tilly for $10,000 in small bills she'd laugh and call the sheriff. Understand?"

I barely understand a single word, but I'm not going to give her the satisfaction. I'll refer you to a corollary to the first rule of foster care: never show weakness. "I understand that the only thing standing between me and an empty bank account is a sheriff who can't manage to stand on his own two feet. Oh, and apparently Tilly simultaneously works at the bank and the diner." I give her a "take that" smirk.

Twiggy looks heavenward and invokes my grandmother. "Myrtle Isadora Johnson Linder Duncan Willamet Rogers, if I didn't think so highly of you I'd run this scrawny idiot out of town before sunset."

All I heard was that she thinks I'm skinny. Nice. Oh, that and the fact that my grandmother had at least five husbands . . .

"Tally works at the diner. Tilly works at the bank. They're sisters. Folks say their parents named each of the kids after the town where he or she was conceived. Now I'm not saying it's an appropriate system, but the oldest sister got made in Tillamook, and goes by Tilly. The youngest got made in Tallahassee, and goes by Tally, and the brother in the middle got cooked up in Toledo, and goes by—"

"Toley," I blurt.

"What the heck kinda name is Toley? No, wiseacre, he goes by Ledo."

I don't believe her for one second. I don't think she liked me stealing her punch line, so she made up the bit about the brother. Regardless, apparently this ornery spinster is my employee, and since I know less than nothing about this place I better make nice. "I'll make a note of those names. Now, would you please walk on over to the bank and get the drawer money. And maybe you can show me around the shop when you get back. Okay?"

Twiggy strides toward the front door and calls back, "Sure enough. I'll show you around the museum and the apartment, too. I s'pose you'll need a place to stay—if you're stayin'." Just before the door closes she adds, "Don't mess with Pyewacket. He ain't a fan of strangers, you know."

The massive door bangs shut behind her, and I make a mental note to get some kind of spring or shock for the unwieldy thing. It's strangely out of place in the brewery-turned-bookshop. The door is intricately decorated with symbols and figures that whisper of faraway places—perhaps my grandmother was a traveler. My gaze returns to the shelves and shelves of books. Reading was my escape from the pain and loss that followed my mother's death. Books contained the only true friends I'd ever known. I smile broadly and close my eyes. I can almost feel the dust in the air, but I inhale deeply regardless of the atoms of paper I'm surely taking in. As I breathe in the energy flowing through the room, there's a noise like someone scratching on metal.

I pop open my eyes and walk toward the sound. There must be a side or rear door. I wander into the back room where Twiggy disappeared earlier and the volume increases.

An illuminated "Exit" sign spills red light into the dim space. As I near the door the scraping becomes clearer. It is definitely an animal. My heart skips a beat. What if my grandmother left me a puppy? I slowly push open the door so I don't hit the hopefully adorable puppy.

Imagine my shock and disappointment when instead of a cuddly bundle of cuteness, I discover a dog-sized alley cat that appears to be half bobcat and half demon! Oh, and it has something nasty in its pointy-toothed mouth. Great! I was hoping to come face to face with a dead mouse today.

I wave my arms to shoo the cat away, but she—or

maybe he—I didn't check under the hood, so let's go with "it." It drops the dead thing on the step and squirts past me into the bookstore in a blur of tan fur and tufted ears that almost knocks me off my feet.

Pyewacket, I assume. Nice to make your acquaintance.

Before my brain can send the "give chase" signal, I inexplicably bend down to get a closer look at the leavings.

"Son of a—" I won't repeat what I actually say. In fact, I won't even tell you what's lying on the step. I run into the bookstore screaming unrepeatables at the cat, who I'm now sure is Pyewacket, while I search for a spoon (ew) or tweezers (yuck) or a dustpan. All I can find are chopsticks.

I demand that the cat get out of my bookshop, and to my great surprise, as I open the side door the demon-spawn feline rockets into the alley.

I pick up the "thing" on the step with the chopsticks and fiercely fight my gag reflex as I shuffle-run toward the dumpster at the end of the alley.

My fingers are shaking.

The thing is slipping.

I am less than a foot from the finish line and my arm is poised to dump and run.

A car turns down the alley.

BWAAP. BWAAP.

Two quick hoots from a siren. Hooray.

Red and blue lights swirl on and off, filling the alleyway with an unwelcome, and wholly misleading, party-like atmosphere.

I slowly turn toward the intrusion.

"I thought that was you," he says.

Sheriff Too Hot To Handle is back for seconds.

"Freeze."

Did he just pull a gun on me?

"Don't take another step." He inches closer. "And drop the— Is that an eyeball?"

Clearly the sheriff is not as thoughtful as me. I'm sorry you had to hear it that way.

I nod and smile. What else can I do?

"Drop the eyeball," he repeats. "And step away from the body."

<u>Buy Fries and Alibis to serve up the guilty today!</u>

A SNEAK PEEK FROM MOLLY
FROM KITTY CONFIDENTIAL

This talking cat has a murder to solve... But will his new human agree to play Watson to his Sherlock?

I was just your normal twenty-something with seven associate degrees and no idea what I wanted to do with my life. That is, until I died... Well, almost.

As if a near-death experience at the hands of an old coffeemaker wasn't embarrassing enough, I woke up to find I could talk to animals. Or rather one animal in particular.

His full name is Octavius Maxwell Ricardo Edmund Frederick Fulton, but since that's way too long for anyone to remember, I've taken to calling him Octo-Cat. He talks so fast he can be difficult to understand, but seems to be telling me that his late owner didn't die of natural causes like everyone believes.

Well, now it looks like I no longer have a choice, apparently my life calling is to serve as Blueberry Bay's first ever pet whisperer P.I while maintaining my façade as a paralegal at the offices of Fulton, Thompson & Associates.

I just have one question: *How did Dr. Dolittle make this gig look so easy?*

KITTY CONFIDENTIAL is now available.

***CLICK HERE* to get your copy so that you can start reading this series today.**

You can also turn the page to read the first chapter... Enjoy!

READ THIS HILARIOUS SNEAK PEEK

I woke up on the conference room floor. Funny, I couldn't remember passing out, yet there I was.

My heart womped a million miles an hour, but most of my body had become fuzzy and tingly. I tried to move my arms, but they seemed content to lay splayed out at my sides. One by one, my senses started to come back online.

Pop!

Mrs. Fulton's shriek was the first thing I heard, then others in the room began to murmur amongst themselves. Some voices I recognized, but others were completely unfamiliar.

Bethany said, "It's probably time we threw that old thing out."

Mr. Fulton ignored her as he rushed toward me. "Angie... Angie..." His panicked voice grew closer until he'd arrived right at my side. "Are you okay?"

Meanwhile, Mr. Thompson mumbled something about liabilities and workman's compensation—exactly as anyone who knew him would expect him to do in such a situation.

I was still trying to remember what had happened when an unexpected weight pressed down onto my chest and made it quite difficult for me to breathe.

The overpowering smell of tuna filled my nostrils, and the sudden intensity of it brought on a coughing fit.

A voice I'd never heard before hovered over me. "Well, how about that? This one had more than one life, after all. People, *pssh*. So fragile."

"Oh, she's breathing!" Diane shouted.

"Of course, she's breathing, honey," her husband responded with a note of relief in his previously panicked voice. "She's also coughing."

"And here I thought the car trip wouldn't be worth it," that same unfamiliar voice chimed in, pairing the words with an unkind chuckle. "That was, paws down, the best entertainment I've had all week."

Finally, my eyes flew open, and I found a gleaming amber gaze watching me from just a few inches away. Wait… Why was there a cat in the office, and why was it *on me*? I struggled to sit up, but my limbs were still too heavy to lift on my own.

"Oh, honey," that voice drawled again. "If you expect to keep walking, then you probably should have landed on your feet."

I let out a loud groan. I could feel the activity humming all around me, but the only thing I saw was the danged cat who was definitely intruding in my personal space right about then.

"What happened?" I asked before coughing again.

"I think the coffeemaker electrocuted you when you tried to plug it in," Diane revealed. Her shaky voice made it obvious she'd been crying. I felt so bad that my clumsiness put her through that.

"Oh, jeez. This one's even stupider than the first. I'm really looking forward to living with her while the rest of the family figures out where to dump me. Such a pity. They don't know greatness when it's staring them in the face."

I moaned and attempted to lift my head to get a better look around the room. "Who is that?" I demanded.

"It's me, Angie," Mrs. Fulton said, squeezing one of my hands in earnest. "You asked what happened, and I told you about the coffeemaker."

"No, the guy who just called both of us stupid." I wished I could sit up to see past this annoying cat, but he was the only thing that filled my vision in that moment. Of course, I had lots of questions about the coffeemaker and how such a tiny old appliance had managed to zap me unconscious, but the need to identify the unknown speaker weighed on me much more heavily.

A cruel snicker sounded nearby. "I called you stupid, because you *are* stupid. Honesty is the best policy, the truth will set you free, yada yada, and all that other nonsense you humans like to say."

If I hadn't known any better, I'd have sworn that strange, lilting voice was coming from the cat. Man, how hard had I hit my head when I fell?

The cat leaned in so close that his whiskers tickled my face. His unnervingly large eyes moved frantically from side to side as if stalking some kind of prey. Oh, how I hoped I wasn't that prey. I'd barely escaped the coffeemaker. If something sentient set out to hurt me today, I wouldn't even stand a chance.

"Did you... Did you really hear what I said?" the voice asked again, and again it really sounded like it was coming from the cat. Did he eat a tiny human or something? None of this made any sense.

"Yes, I hear you, and I think you're rather mean," I answered with a huff, giving the best attitude I could, considering my prone position.

"Angie, who are you talking to?" Diane asked with words that sounded unsure and just as worried as I felt myself.

"I'm not sure who it is, but he keeps insulting me." I closed my eyes tight, then slowly opened them again.

The cat seemed to smile, but not in a friendly way. Once again, I wondered if he considered me easy prey. Heck, I considered me easy prey, too.

"No one's insulting you," Mr. Fulton insisted. "We all just want to make sure you're okay."

The cat smiled again, bigger this time. "Ooh, ooh, me! I'm insulting you, you big, stupid bag of skin."

"He just called me a big, stupid bag of skin! Can you really not hear him?" I blinked half a dozen times, then pinched myself. Nothing seemed to change.

"Russo, I think maybe you should take the rest of the day off and a trip to the emergency room," Mr. Thompson commanded after clearing his throat loudly from somewhere near the door.

"Wow, you really can hear me," the voice said again. "By the way, hi, I'm Octavius Maxwell Ricardo Edmund Frederick Fulton, and I have some demands."

I was having a difficult time keeping track of all the threads of conversation. I knew the partners were worried about me and about themselves, but I still couldn't identify the mystery speaker or figure out what he wanted. "Octavius Maxwell... who?"

"Honey, are you talking about the cat?" Mrs. Fulton asked, picking the tabby off from my chest.

My straining lungs thanked her, and immediately I felt stronger.

In a cutesy baby voice, Diane held the cat up to her face and cooed, "Are you trying to help our Angie feel better? You're such a sweet fuzzy wuzzy."

The cat turned to me and narrowed his eyes into slits. *"Heeeeelp meeeee."*

Energized at last by my need to find out what the heck was going on, I managed to sit up and look around the room.

"Oh, good. Now that you can move again, Peters will take you to the hospital," Thompson decreed.

Bethany sighed but didn't argue the point.

"Wait!" The tabby cat trotted up to me the second Diane set him back on the floor. "What about my demands?"

I stared at him, dumbfounded. There was absolutely no way...

The cat flicked his tail and emitted a low growl from deep in his throat. "I know you can hear me, so how about doing the polite thing and keeping up your end of the conversation, huh?"

"What do you want?" I whispered, but still everyone in the office could see and hear the crazy lady talking to the cat she'd just met.

"My owner was murdered, and I need you to

help me prove it. Also, of equal importance, I haven't been fed in hours. Maybe years." His ears fell back against his head and his eyes widened, making me feel inexplicably fond of him despite his bad attitude.

Then the first part of what he said hit me, and I gasped. *"Murdered?"*

Bethany tittered nervously and grabbed me by the arm. "Okay, let's get you to the hospital. Hallucinations are not a good sign."

"But…" I began to argue. That argument fell away when I realized I had no sane or valid reason to resist.

"Murdered!" the cat shouted after me dramatically. "She was offed before her time, and now that I know you can hear me, you're going to help me get her the justice she deserves. It's the least I can do to thank her for all the years she spent feeding me and arranging my pillows just as I like them. Also, did you hear the part about me needing to be fed?"

Bethany and I had almost made it to the doorway. That meant it was my last chance to talk to the cat. For all I knew, we would never see each other again. Of course, I knew it was totally crazy to assume there was even a chance any of this being real, but still, I couldn't ignore the fact that the talking tabby needed my help.

"I want to help!" I bellowed back into the room just before the door closed behind us.

"No, you *need* help," Bethany growled, sounding even more like an animal than the cat had. "Thanks a lot, by the way. This was the first time they've included me in something this important to the firm. Now, thanks to your little act with the coffeemaker, I'm going to miss it."

That hurt almost as bad as the zap from the coffeemaker. "You honestly don't think I electrocuted myself just to sabotage you, do you?"

She sighed and pinched the bridge of her nose. "No, I'm sorry. I know it's not your fault. I just have to work twice as hard to get ahead since I'm the only female associate, and everyone wants to put me on the baby track instead of the partner track."

"Yeah, well... at least you're not just some glorified secretary." I honestly couldn't believe Bethany was complaining about *her* problems when I'd just had a near-death experience a few minutes earlier...

Or maybe I could. It was Bethany, after all.

She settled me into the passenger seat of her car. It was a newer model Lexus, which told me she probably didn't have things quite as bad as she thought. Still, I felt guilty for costing her what she considered to be her big shot, so I said, "For what it's worth, you're the smartest one of them all."

She laughed as she buckled her seatbelt and adjusted the rear-view mirror. "Even more than Thompson and Fulton?"

I nodded, and the movement made me dizzy. "Especially more than Thompson and Fulton."

We shared a brief glance of camaraderie before she backed out of her spot and navigated onto the main road. Hopefully there would be no more trains passing through today, because despite our brief bond of sisterhood, I wasn't sure how long either of us could handle being trapped in a car together.

"Thanks for taking me, even though I know you didn't want to. You don't have to wait around. Just drop me off and I'll call my nan to come get me when I'm done."

"Already planned on it. If I hurry, I can still make part of the reading." She tapped at her temple to once again show her superior thinking.

And just like that, we were back to normal.

As for me? I wasn't so sure.

KITTY CONFIDENTIAL is now available.

CLICK HERE to get your copy so that you can start reading this series today.

ABOUT TRIXIE SILVERTALE

Trixie Silvertale grew up reading an endless supply of Lilian Jackson Braun, Hardy Boys, and Nancy Drew novels. She loves the amateur sleuths in cozy mysteries and obsesses about all things paranormal. Those two passions unite in her paranormal cozy mystery series, and she's thrilled to write them and share them with you.

When she's not consumed by writing, she bakes to fuel her creative engine and pulls weeds in her herb garden to clear her head (*and sometimes she pulls out her hair, but mostly weeds*).

If you're looking for more from Trixie Silvertale, sign up for her monthly newsletter at **trixiesilvertale.com/paranormal-cozy-club-2/**

Greetings are welcome:
trixie@trixiesilvertale.com
Bookbub | **Facebook** | **Instagram**

Click here to **Join Trixie's Club!**

A NOTE FROM TRIXIE

I've always been a huge fan of haunted mansions...

The best part of "living" in Misty Meadows was the chance to build a brand new world, and meet Sydney Coleman and Sir Bogart. And big "spooky" hugs to the world's best ARC Team – Trixie's Mystery ARC Detectives!

It was an honor and a pleasure to work with Molly Fitz and Whiskered Mysteries. They offered me the opportunity to step into a wonderful new tale, for a book or three, and I loved it.

I'm especially grateful for the helpful architecture info provided by Michael. Thanks to Josh and Morgan for making me watch scary movies!

FUN FACT: I once toured the home of a famous Hollywood stunt coordinator and it had a secret room!

SECRET: I'm obsessed with caramel-apple cupcakes.

Thank you for visiting Moonlight Manor.

TRIXIE SILVERTALE (SEPTEMBER 2022)

MITZY MOON MYSTERIES

A gift that's too good to be true. A murder she didn't commit. A barista in a latte trouble...

Mitzy Moon believes she's an orphan, so she's dumbstruck when a special delivery to her low-rent apartment reveals a family. But her shock turns to awe when she discovers her grandmother left her a fortune, a fiendish feline, and a bookshop of rare tomes brimming with magic. Start with Book 1: **Fries and Alibis**.

MAGICAL RENAISSANCE FAIRE MYSTERIES

A dubious festival. A fatal swim. Can this fortune-telling fairy herald the true killer?

Coriander the Conjurer is trapped in a cursed Renaissance Faire, but that's the good news. Her usual routine of reading patrons' futures and compensating for her lopsided fairy wings is interrupted when a scuffle turns deadly. Now, in order to broker peace within the realm she must solve a mermaid's murder. But she'll need the help of a dangerous vampire and her meddling toad familiar to uncover the real clues. Start the adventure with **All Swell That Ends Spell.**

ABOUT MOLLY FITZ

While *USA Today bestselling* author Molly Fitz can't technically talk to animals, she and her three feline writing assistants have deep and very animated conversations as they navigate their days.

She lives with her husband, child, and their own private zoo somewhere in the wilds of Alaska. Molly will occasionally venture out for good food, great coffee, or to meet new animal friends.

Learn more about Molly and her books, and be sure to sign up for her newsletter at **www.MollyMysteries.com**.

ALSO BY MOLLY FITZ

Learn more about Molly's collected works, so that you can decide which book you'd like to read next…

PET WHISPERER P.I.

Angie Russo just partnered up with Blueberry Bay's first ever talking cat detective. Along with his ragtag gang of human and animal helpers, Octo-Cat is determined to save the day... so long as it doesn't interfere with his schedule.

Start with book 1, **Kitty Confidential**.

MERLIN'S MAGICAL MYSTERIES

Gracie Springs is not a witch... but her cat is. Now she must help to keep his secret or risk spending the rest of her life in some magical prison. Too bad trouble seems to find them at every turn!

Start with book 1, **Merlin Takes a Familiar**.

PARANORMAL TEMP AGENCY

Tawny Bigford's simple life takes a turn for the magical when she stumbles upon her landlady's murder and is recruited by a talking black cat named Fluffikins to take over the deceased's role as the official Town Witch for Beech Grove, Georgia.

Start with book 1, **Witch for Hire**.

THE MYSTERIES OF MOONLIGHT MANOR (WITH TRIXIE SILVERTALE)

Sydney Coleman has it all—until she doesn't. No sooner does she launch her bed and breakfast, than a trio of ghosts turn up oppose her at every turn. They insist she solve the murder of their mistress, but Sydney is desperate for cash. If she can't book some guests fast, her haunted mansion is utterly doomed.

Start with book 1, ***Moonlight & Mischief***.

CONNECT WITH MOLLY

Sign up for my newsletter and get a special digital prize pack for joining, including an exclusive story, *Meowy Christmas Mayhem*, fun quiz, and lots of cat pictures!

Sign up: **MollyMysteries.com/subscribe**

Now, if you ever wished you could converse with cats, here's your opportunity! This is me officially inviting you into my whacky inner world as part of my Cozy Kitty Book Club.

For those who just can't get enough of my zany cat characters and their hapless humans, this book club will provide new content to devour and the chance to get to know my best author friends.

From exclusive stories, behind-the-scenes trivia to never-before-released bonus content, and monthly giveaways, there's a lot to love about the Cozy Kitty

Book Club. Join today to find out what we're reading next!

Join: **MollyMysteries.com/club**

Printed in Dunstable, United Kingdom